Gulsifat Shakhidi

FARKHOD

FROM NAVGHILEM

LONDON
2021

English-Russian

Published in the United Kingdom
Hertfordshire Press Ltd. 2021
E-mail: publisher@hertfordshirepress.com
www.hertfordshirepress.com

FARKHOD FROM NAVGHILEM
by Gulsifat Shakhidi

English-Russian

Russian version Edited by Vera Deynichenko
Translated by Tatiana F. Kinzhalova
English language editor: Stephen M. Bland
Illustration: Maria Averyanova
Typeset: Alexandra Rey
Project management: Angelina Krasnogir

ISBN: 978-1-913356-36-1

CONTENTS

Humour Helps Us to Live

Gulsifat Shakhidi has prepared an unexpected gift for her readers and admirers, the humorous tale, Farkhod from Navghilem. This time her heroes are not women and children, but three inseparable male friends: Farkhod, Abdulvasi and Faridun.

The fellow countrymen from the mountain village of Navghilem firmly believe in themselves, and were steadily bringing to fruition their unpretentious dreams of attaining a higher education, building a house, and calmly and raising a family with their beloved wives. Those happy plans were destroyed by the fierce, fratricidal civil war in Tajikistan of 1990-1993.

In my devastated native Republic, specialists with a higher education were no longer needed anywhere, and in order to provide for their families, the friends had to join the swelling army of migrants. Farkhod and Abdulvasi began to drive cars from Germany to Russia, and their adventures are described in G. Shakhidi's story, 'Faberjuve's Revenge' in a style which can be described as 'laughing through the tears.' Faridun, meanwhile, becomes 'registered' at some construction sites in Moscow and the Moscow Region, and tries to apply the skills he acquires in the improvement of his friends' houses (the story, 'Sunlight Dogs').

In different life situations, the heroes of the piece do not lose heart. On the contrary, they bounteously accompany conversations and arguments with jokes and funny stories shared with the good people around them who happen to be displaced from their native lands (in the stories 'Five Minutes before Take-off,' 'The Old Man, Khottabych,' 'The First Blow is Half the Battle,' and 'Tsar Cauldron'). Farkhod, Abdulvasi and Faridun are able to admit to their mistakes, to get out of trouble with dignity and be the first to laugh at themselves (the stories 'Hold the Thief!', 'The Sun on Credit,' and 'A Gathering of 'Minas' on the BMW').

I have intentionally not disclosed the plots of the stories written by Gulsifat Shakhidi, so as not to deprive readers of the novelty of her gift of perception. Still, I cannot help but decipher the fact of personal character. Gulsifat named one of the heroes of the story, Gleb Nikolayevich, and invented the surname 'Dobrov'. This is a tribute to the memory of my late husband, Gleb Nikolayevich Deynichenko, a graduate of the Philological Faculty of the Tajik State University, a journalist, poet and author. His famous words-spoonerisms are put into the mouths of Farkhod and Abdulvasi. I am immensely grateful to Gulya for this, because everyone who knew Gleb Deinichenko will remember him fondly once again upon reading the story and his poems.

The new heroes of Gulsifat Shakhidi's fiction have not grown hard-hearted in these difficult times. Humour helps them to brighten their lives and adjust their relationships with the wider public. I truly hope that readers will like the guys from Navghilem, and come to include them in their network of friends.

Vera Deynichenko,
journalist.

Let's Get Acquainted

My name is Farkhod. I'm an ordinary guy from the beautiful mountain village of Navghilem in the north of Tajikistan. In our neighbourhood many Uzbeks lived, who did not pronounce the letter 'F.' Therefore, throughout my childhood my name was 'Parkhod,' or even 'Parokhod,' (meaning 'steamboat' in Russian). As my childhood passed and I became an adult, everyone stopped distorting my name, thank God. Just imagine what they called my friend, Faridun – 'Paridun,' 'Pardon,' and so on. He was the sixth son in the family, and when he was born his father came home drunk and hollered in the yard, 'Only sons from me!' After that, as evil tongues spoke in all the families where only girls had been born, suddenly, boys looking like their neighbour began to be engendered.

But it's better we talk about me. There are three sons in my family, and I am the youngest, the same age as Faridun (this is why no one would think anything bad).

The story of my name, 'Farkhod' is very interesting, and Mom never tired of repeating it in every way possible. Next to my great aunt there lived a family who had eleven children. All their names began with the letter 'F.' They called the youngest children unusual names for Tajiks: Fidel, Flora, Frida, and one of the older sisters was Farida. When I was born, our great aunt visited us. She was old and wise, and decided to name me 'Farkhod.' She explained to my mother that in her neighbour's large family she liked Farkhod the most as he was the smartest, kindest and most polite of the children. I still ask myself the question: 'What if Fidel had been the best? Oh, how would I have lived with that name?'

We, the children of the time of the senseless civil war of the 90s in Tajikistan, somehow became grown-ups very quickly. After I graduated from secondary school and then high school, following the example of my friends I went to Russia as a labour migrant. I married my classmate, the beautiful Latofat rather early. She was my first love. At that time, we decided not to have children until after we graduated, but, as they say, 'we assume and God disposes.' Upon the completion of my studies, two children were already born: my daughter, Laylo, and my son, Oraz. I realised, therefore, that I needed to go and earn good money in order to support them.

Since childhood, I often sat behind the steering wheel of my father's car and drove along with him. When I grew up, despite my father's prohibitions, I drove in secret by myself, although I was afraid of his anger. One day, a wheel fell into a canal, and I had to call people for help. They pulled out the car, and I quietly drove it home. There wasn't even a scratch on it.

The next day, my father left on business, and the pressure dropped in the wheel. No matter how hard he tried to pull out the spare, he couldn't do it. It turned out that when I flew into the canal, the car was so jammed the spare tyre became 'glued' to the boot. My father couldn't comprehend it, but I immediately realised what had happened and pretended to be surprised. Practice made me a good driver, and at age sixteen I got a driving license in a distant area by redoing my birth certificate to say I was eighteen. So here I was, a young up-and-comer.

My first job as a labour migrant was related to driving cars from Europe to my native Tajikistan. By driving such distances, as you might imagine, my level of practice behind the wheel was rich, so over time I became considered an ace. We travelled in pairs as co-drivers to support each other on the road. My friend Abdulvasi, or simply "Vasya," had driven cars several times, but only from Russia, so we decided to go to Germany ourselves so as not to overpay for many services. However, we were out of pocket, and the reason why you will understand.

Revenge of Faberjuve
FABERJUVE'S EGGS

Do not be surprised; I am a well-educated person and do not think I have made a mistake. It's not the story of the famous Faberge - the manufacturer of precious bejewelled eggs - but about ordinary chicken eggs. Now I'll tell you everything in detail. My life could not go on without constant adventures.

Our first trip to Germany began very smoothly. In the suburbs of Potsdam there was a place for scrapping old cars, which, due to their condition, had been sent for recycling. At the outstation, they knew that "former Soviet" people came to buy used cars, and therefore tried to assemble cars of the same brand almost like new with normal performance using the parts from old ones. They sold them, and it was all perfectly legal. My friend and I chose a car; it was exactly the type we wanted. Having arranged the documents and paid for everything, we drove back after two days filled with joy. How punctual the Germans are, and how many people could learn a lot from them!

Upon approaching the border of the former Soviet Union, we soon felt the difference. In Kaunas, Lithuania, we were the first to reach customs clearance. To our delight there were parking places right next to the point, and we immediately parked our car at the front, not paying attention to the fact that many other cars were standing idle in the distance.

Suddenly, we saw an old man of small stature behind the low lattice of the parking lot. He smiled at us so sweetly. We greeted him, and he laughed. I told Vasya that his sly smile and small, half-closed eyes reminded me of Commissaire Juve, the character played by the actor Louis de Funès in the French film, Fantômas. The old man turned to us and we saw a slingshot in his hands. We laughed, and then we went for a snack and to look for a place to stay overnight, as it would be necessary to return early the next morning.

Rejoicing that we would be the first to go through all the customs procedures, we ate and fell asleep. In the morning, we ran to customs; and what did we see? The whole car was as if painted a dirty yellow colour and it shone brightly in the first rays of the sun. At first we thought that someone had changed the car, but when we came closer we were seized with terror. There were broken EGGS all over the car! Yes, real raw chicken eggs! Twisting the slingshot in his hands, the old man from the day before looked at us with a smile from the house opposite.

We ran to the customs office to find out what had happened to our car. The answer was simple: everyone there already knew that old troublemaker and never left cars in front of his house. He had a lot of hens and was renowned for making mischief, and because he had a psychiatrist's note, no amount of persuasion could persuade the police to help.

'Why didn't you tell us about this yesterday?' we asked.

'Well, you wanted to go first, so now you'll have to wait as long as is necessary.'

With a sigh, we reserved a place in the queue and went to a specialised washing station according to the address indicated by the customs officers. Apparently, there was a secret work contract going on there.

What one broken egg is you can certainly imagine, but when almost a hundred had been broken and dried? Washing the car ourselves would be like making scrambled eggs, and the glued shells would do their onerous job. So, we had to spend money on the best wash available, where we were met with loud laughter. It turned out the whole of Kaunas knew about our old man. I became restless and resentful; I had been so glad we had saved money, and now we had to spend double and, moreover, to wait for another day.

When we had finally passed customs, we stopped at the house of "Commissaire Juve" to find out why he'd punished us so badly. He smiled, examined his slingshot, and then said in a sly manner:

'Now you will remember Uncle Faber for a long time.'

'We will remember you for life, dear Commissaire Faberjuve,' I answered.

'Well, well, that means now you'll keep your cars away from my house.'

Uncle Faber opened his little running eyes with satisfaction and turned away with a roguish grin. In his hands behind his back, he toyed with the slingshot.

Many years have passed, but Abdulvasi - Vasya and I like to tell friends this story about Faberjuve's eggs. Now, I have shared it with you, too.

Sunlight Dogs

After five years of migrant labour activity, I managed to save some money and bought an old three-room apartment in a brick house in downtown Khojent. A German family used to live there, but had moved away because of the civil war. The apartment was a sight for sore eyes. The Germans could only be praised for their accuracy and thrift. I was very glad to settle in the micro-district neighbouring my friends, Faridun and Abdulvasi. The only drawback of the apartment was the ground floor and the absence of grates on the windows. The years were turbulent, so before my next scheduled departure I decided to put grates on the windows.

I asked my friends where I could find a good workman.

'Uh, don't worry,' Faridun replied, 'we'll come up with something ourselves.'

He understood all that stuff as he'd worked on a construction site near Moscow.

'They have left a lot of armature at an abandoned construction site,' Abdulvasi added enterprisingly. 'We'll take it away as it's all ownerless.'

'Then what?' I asked.

'We'll ask someone how it's done; they'll show us and then we'll make it ourselves. After all, aren't we three skilful men?' Faridun assured me. 'Firstly, we need reinforcement, and it is lying right under your nose. Secondly, we need a gas bottle and a welding machine. Thirdly, we need a sketch, or rather a draft, well, in general, a drawing.'

'It's obvious that you graduated from the Polytechnical Institute, because you feel like drawing all the drafts,' Abdulvasi interrupted. 'Lattices are lattices; it's not like we're putting them up in a theatre.'

'Not in a theatre, of course, but still, it' not like in a prison!' Faridun protested.

'Listen, firstly, secondly, thirdly, in a theatre, in a prison - I'm tired of it!' I stopped them. 'We have tickets and tomorrow we'll fly to Moscow, so there's no time for disputes.'

'Then cut them out of cardboard, Farkhod, it's quick and without any problems,' Faridun grumbled in an offended voice.

We decided that Abdulvasi and I would go to the construction site for the fittings, and Faridun would get the rest.

It was quiet at the abandoned construction site as we approached the pile of building material. We began to load a trolley with fittings and immediately figured out how much we needed for two windows and a large veranda. We finished loading and decided to head back, but we had another thing coming. It was as if a watchman had appeared in front of us in the form of a huge dog. It seemed to be wagging its tail peacefully, so we made to go around him, but he would not let us pass. What to do? It turned out the owners of the construction site had abandoned everything, even their dog. Now it became clear why no one touched the building materials.

I called Faridun (long live mobile phones), explained everything and asked him to buy liverwurst sausages, take sleeping pills from my wife, and rush to our aid. Latofat understood nothing, but knowing my eccentricities, she gave him the pills.

Soon, Faridun came running up and fed the dog. It gladly ate the sausage and began to fall asleep. We left Faridun with him and hurried to the house with our heavy load. Faridun shouted to us that he had brought a master welder, and he was waiting with his equipment.

An hour passed before we found out what had happened to the "watchman." It turned out that the sleeping pills were only effective on such a large dog for fourteen minutes. Faridun tried to distract him and then climbed a tree. No, the dog did not bite him; some kids came to feed the dog, and it went after them instead. Having climbed so high up the tree in his panic, Faridun couldn't get down and fell, hitting himself on the branches. He was ragged from head to toe. He was lucky, however, compared to what happened to us. Listen up!

Without waiting for Faridun, Abdulvasi and I talked to the welder and started to work. The welder made the frames, and we stood nearby and "composed" a modest window ornament. The welding machine buzzed and sparks flew in all directions, but we looked at him and did not understand why the welder had such huge sunglasses. Once he was finished, we fixed the window grates into place at once.

For the veranda, it turned out to be twice as much work. I wanted something unusual, but alas, I am not an artist. As for the welder, it was irrelevant to him; he just did what we said whilst constantly asking us to stand farther away. We were offended he kept shooing us away, but an hour later we were already installing a large grid on the veranda.

At that point, Faridun arrived all shredded and battered. We burst out laughing and he, peering into our eyes, anxiously asked:

'Have you been watching the welding without special protective glasses? Here, you are the fools! You have caught so many "sunlight dogs" ('bunnies' according to a Russian saying) that you won't be in Moscow for two weeks!'

Waving a hand at us, he went to tend to his wounds.

We didn't understand anything about the "sunlight dogs," paid the money to the welder, and decided to rest before tomorrow's flight to Moscow. Work always awaits labour migrants.

Words can barely describe what happened next. That night my eyes were swollen so badly, it was impossible to even open them. We called an ambulance, and I was taken to a medical department specialising in eyes, where my partner, Abdulvasi was already waiting.

Our wives returned our tickets. We were in the hospital for a week, and for another week we had to be treated in a clinic. The ophthalmologist, our attending physician, joked all the time, 'Well, do you want to catch some more "sunlight dogs?"'

The lattice on my veranda turned out to be such a messy "pattern" that not just a child, but an adult could easily climb through it in some places. What were all those sacrifices for; we almost lost our eyes!

Now I know what welding is. It would have been better if Abdulvasi and I had worked on a construction site as Faridun did instead of driving cars.

That's the story of the "sunlight dogs."

Hold the Thief!

Abdulvasi and I drove cars from Germany to Russia on numerous occasions before deciding to buy one for ourselves. We thought we would arrange the documents at the Moscow taxi depot, and keep busy driving a taxi in shifts. The seller in Germany was aware of our position during our "business," and assembled a very bright, beautiful, almost new car. As a taxi, it was high class.

Without queuing or obstacles, we got a job, either because our documents and driving experience were in perfect order, or our radiant BMW took their fancy.

One day, I gave a lift from Sheremetyevo Airport to an oligarch who was in a hurry to get to a meeting and didn't want to wait for his car, which was stuck in a traffic jam. I delivered my passenger swiftly, and he asked for my business card, expressing his satisfaction and noting that he needed such drivers.

As he got out of the car, he took off his raincoat and I saw his shirt, which looked just like my Uncle Tahir's shirt. I had seen those blue and white speckles only once - twenty years ago when I came to Dushanbe as a teenager. That reminded me of the story of my uncle's shirts.

My uncle, a famous and talented journalist, was known as a fashionista. Well, he had such a job and was responsible for events, meetings, interviews and so on. My father and uncle were not very much alike; it was as if they came from different families. My father called his brother an 'aesthete,' and for a long time I didn't understand why, until I saw everything with my own eyes.

One day, Uncle Tahir went to Spain under the protection of the Society for Friendship with Foreign Countries, but at his own expense. At that time, I stayed with them during my winter vacation. My Aunt Saodat, my Cousin Timur and I enjoyed walking around Dushanbe, which was decorated for the New Year celebrations and shining with colourful lights. The school holidays were extended for a whole month in that military year of 1991.

Ten days quickly passed before Uncle Tahir returned, feeling very pleased with himself. We were all expecting presents. He gave me a set of postcards with views of Barcelona, and Timur got a transparent glass souvenir with a view of the capital of Spain - Madrid. When the souvenir was turned over, it snowed, but the tiny figurines of the people remained in their summer clothes. I don't remember what Uncle Tahir presented his wife, Saodat with, but he showed off with great pleasure fifteen men's shirts which he'd purchased for himself.

'There are no shirts like this here!' he kept repeating, his eyes shining with pride and delight.

Indeed, the shirts really were incomparable. In those years of total deficit, it was simply impossible to get anything of the kind. Each shirt seemed better than the last: coloured ones with a white collar, blue speckled ones, stripes, polka dots, ones with ruffles - you could not list all of them. I had never seen such a thing. My uncle could not admire them for long, however, as soon the following happened.

Uncle Tahir changed his Spanish shirt every day for the sake of smartness. When he took one off, he hung it on a chair - as if he couldn't part with them even for washing - put on a new one and went to work. Only on the fifteenth day, he requested his wife wash them by hand. Having performed the task neatly, Aunt Saodat wanted to dry them on the veranda because it had been snowing the day before, and in the morning everything melted and flowed from the roofs and trees in the warm sun. Uncle Tahir, though, decided to hang the subjects of his pride in the street in the fresh air. He tied a clothesline away from the drops and hung all fifteen shirts. No matter how much my aunt tried to dissuade him as they could be stolen, it was as if my uncle did not hear her. He sat down in his office by the window and began to write a new interview whilst simultaneously watching his shirts.

Fifteen minutes later, my aunt was preparing dinner in the kitchen and Timur and I were playing checkers in the nursery when we heard my uncle cursing in his office, and saw him storm into the street. We rushed after him, followed by the startled Aunt Saodat.

'What's happened?!! Why...' she began, and then she froze.

The clothesline was empty.

'Imagine, some bastards have stolen fifteen shirts in fifteen minutes,' he growled, the first time I had heard such nasty words from my gallant uncle, an aesthete, in essence.

'But I warned you,' my aunt reproached him.

My uncle waved his hand in frustration and was silent for the whole evening, except for sighing heavily. Not long had he been able to enjoy his Spanish shirts. But this was not the end of the story, for three days later he returned from the editorial office in a triumphant mood.

'Imagine, I've found the thief,' he told us cheerfully. 'I went to a store to buy bread, and right in front of me there was a guy in my shirt! I stopped him and asked where he got it, and the guy got scared.'

'Do you know who I am?' my uncle asked the thief. 'I am a famous journalist; the whole Republic knows me. Do you have all the shirts?'

'Yes, please excuse me. I will return everything,' the fellow answered guiltily.

Uncle Tahir asked the thief how long it would take to get the shirts back, and the guy assured him he would be at the entrance of the house in fifteen minutes.

'Timur, Farkhod, come with me and let's wait on the bench together,' our uncle invited us.

'Who catches a thief like that? Did you believe him? You should have taken him by the collar and dragged him to the police station. You should have taken your shirt off him as evidence and presented it to the law enforcement agencies. Did you even ask what his name is or where he lives?!! No? Now look, you can whistle for it! He has escaped, and his trail has gone cold,' Aunt Saodat laughed.

'How badly you think of people,' my uncle reproached her naively.

'I believe in people, but not thieves,' my aunt answered in an offended tone. 'He has robbed you, deceived you, and now he'll be rejoicing that he's got off so easily. Now sit and wait until pigs fly. Maybe then, all the shirts will return.'

We had been standing at the entrance for almost two hours. It was completely dark and freezing cold. Uncle Tahir kept looking towards the store where he'd caught the thief. Then, my aunt could stand it no more and ushered us inside saying that the wait could last for many years, or even a lifetime. She joked that the thief was a 'nice guy,' because at least he'd apologised for the theft, but my uncle remained downcast.

Nowadays, he remembers that incident and tells it to his friends as an anecdote, laughing heartily with everyone. Sometimes, I think that in my eccentricities and gullibility, I am very similar to Uncle Tahir. Now, when I meet Aunt Saodat, to my question, 'How are you?' she replies cheerfully:

'Everything is very good, only now we are still waiting for our thief with the Spanish shirts. Probably, though, he's already worn them out.'

Do you know what I was thinking about while looking at the oligarch in a Spanish shirt in my taxi? "Couldn't he and his accomplices have been the ones who stole my uncle's favourite shirts from the clothesline back then; could he?'

A Gathering of 'Mina' Birds on the BMW

Do you remember, my friends, the oligarch I was telling you about who I gave a lift from the airport who was wearing a Spanish shirt exactly like the one belonging to my Uncle Tahir? My uncle's fifteen shirts were stolen from a clothesline in the street, and I wondered whether my passenger had participated in that crime. I didn't have the spirit to ask him point-blank, however. Moreover, my passenger liked me, and we even exchanged business cards just in case.

The oligarch was called Gleb Nikolayevich. You won't believe me, but he phoned and offered me work as a driver in his campaign. He asked whether I could find a co-driver, and all that at a time when Abdulvasi and I desperately needed something in life to change.

At that time, Faridun had invited us to Khojent to be present at the thuy (ritual circumcision of his baby) celebrations. He requested that we arrive in the BMW because it looked like a real 'general's' car. It should be known by everyone what kind of car he would arrive at the restaurant in. Is it laughable? It was definitely funny for us, but for him it was important. He even dreamt of buying that car from us.

Abdulvasi and I wanted to support our friend, but we could be left without a job because of the trip to the thuy celebrations. And just at the moment, Gleb Nikolayevich appeared with an enviable proposal. I became utterly speechless in amazement, but it would have been improper to show my feelings, so I said the proposal was interesting and I'd think about it.

'I'll give you a period of two weeks,' Gleb Nikolayevich said in summation.

'Good,' I agreed with restraint, although I was ready to jump up to the ceiling with joy. After all, so many problems could be immediately solved: I would be able to go to the celebrations with my friend, sell the car there, and, most importantly, get a well-paying job.

After the conversation with Gleb Nikolayevich, we both wrote a letter of resignation which was accepted forthwith, as there were many willing drivers. Early in the morning, we were on our way. Four days later, we were gaily greeted by relatives, and especially by the happy Faridun.

Prior to the celebrations, as was customary in such cases, it was necessary to conduct many traditional events, including morning pilaf, the arrival of mahalla elders to bless the ceremony, and much more. As regards the women's ceremonial gatherings, I would have to tell a whole new story since there were many affairs to be taken care of (a woman's work is never done). Therefore, I will stay silent about this.

After such a long journey, we decided to take the car directly to a carwash, because early in the morning we had to go to the pilaf. How it sparkled; all cleaned up, it became even more beautiful! We left the car under a big branchy tree in the yard and went for a rest. I slept uneasily, waking to the incessant chirping of mina birds, as we called Asian starlings.

'Today, the minas probably have some kind of celebration, or "a gathering of production leaders,"' I said to my wife.

She laughed, and I fell asleep again.

At first light the next morning, Abdulvasi woke me. He kept talking and talking about the car, but being too sleepy, I couldn't really understand anything.

'It is such a picture, you don't know whether to laugh or to cry,' my goggle-eyed friend explained.

I became scared and asked:

'What?! Has it been stolen? Have they removed the wheels and broken the windows?'

'Go downstairs and see for yourself; it's unpleasant even to speak of it,' Abdulvasi muttered.

I quickly washed my face, got dressed, and ran down to the car. What did I see? Our handsome BMW was filthy with the droppings of mina birds. No Uncle Faber from Kaunas with his slingshot could have even imagined such carnage; but that was alien territory, and this was our native Khojent. The car was an eerie colour, and the smell was horrible. It was impossible to come close to it, and even standing at a distance was an assault on the senses. Having become aware of the situation, Faridun ran up to us all out of breath.

'Now, guests will start to arrive for oshi nakhor (morning pilaf). I wanted to give some old people a lift in this car. What am I to do?' the host asked in desperation.

'Take another car. There is nothing to be done. You can't scold these minas and make them wash everything, so start your celebrations without us and we'll go to the carwash. What can I say? Our minnushki took a fancy and "washed" the beautiful car in their own way at their "festivities,"' I replied.

I forgot to tell you that my friend Abdulvasi liked to distort words in both Tajik and Russian in a very funny way. He managed to mix them in conversation, and at that moment he pushed his tagiyah (skullcap) to one side and grunted:

'The minnushki didn't wash the car, but vice versa. They were attacked by a hero named Usrak!'

We howled with laughter.

How we got into the car and drove to a chorus of whistles and the laughter of the boys would be difficult to describe. And how much laughter there was at the carwash! The workers didn't even want to wash our BMW for triple the price, but eventually they took pity and asked us to come back in an hour.

We had to go on foot to the morning pilaf, where we were greeted as the heroes of the latif (a humorous story). It turned out that everyone knew what had happened and was joking about it, adding ridiculous details. Some said we had carried sweet gifts, and the birds were too full of food, others said we did it ourselves so no one could put a jinx on our 'general's' car, whilst others still insisted on the machinations of envious people. The morning pilaf was very cheerful, and laughter rang throughout the mahalla (micro-district). Abdulvasi and I also laughed, although we felt like crying.

An hour later, we went to the carwash and drove away in our sparkling car. We returned to the thuy celebrations, and all the guests went out to look at the general's car. One by one, they began to joke:

'Well? Have you brought the car of the chairman for the meeting of minnushki birds?'

'Well, of course, it's a sin not to mention such a car!'

'Faridun, now you will have the most famous car. Legends will be told about it.'

'Don't park it under a tree that's an assembly hall for a meeting of minas!'

Children from all over the mahalla gathered around the BMW and requested we give them a ride.

'Let's go to the meeting of the minnushki. Tonight, they will give a gala concert at dinner time!'

We went to a restaurant together, and at the wheel, Faridun, the new owner of the car, sat proudly. His dream had come true. Friends and neighbours inquired with interest and often with a smile:

'Isn't this the general's car the mina birds washed?'

The Sun on Credit

Our trip to Khojent turned out to be very pleasant. After the circumcision of his son, Faridun decided to surprise everyone, and planned to organise a gushtingiri (a contest of wrestlers) on the days of the festivities. He invited eminent baklava-heroes from our mahalla and other micro-districts of the city, but circumstances can alter cases.

On the evening before the day of the competition, the weather began to change dramatically. Gloomy clouds enveloped the sky, and Faridun became worried:

'If it rains tomorrow, everything will have to be cancelled. There isn't any sports hall nearby, and even with a remote one we'd have had to sign a contract in advance.'

'Well, it's going to clear up, don't worry,' I tried to sooth my friend.

'We'll order special guns to disperse the clouds,' Abdulvasi joked.

'You make jokes after I've paid for everything? I don't want to disappoint the participants; Sultan-hero himself promised to come, and people want to see him,' Faridun continued in despair.

'If he's a real fighter, neither snow nor rain will hinder him,' I said.

'He will surely come, but who will watch? It's not very pleasant to even stand in the rain, and competing in the mud is not cool for baklava wrestlers!' Abdulvasi said, adding fuel to the fire.

'Okay. As they say, tomorrow is another day. Let's hope for good weather,' Faridun mumbled, looking sadly at the sky.

We were getting ready to go home when Faridun's wife, Nasiba came running up to us. Almost out of breath, she said that at the women's gathering a neighbour had shared the news that Khairullo, a domullo (the minister of a mosque) who lived in a nearby micro-district, could beseech God for good weather. Abdulvasi and I laughed so hard we were probably heard throughout the whole mahalla, but Faridun asked his wife with hope:

'Have you found out where he lives? Do you know his address?'

I exchanged glances with Abdulvasi and burst out laughing again.

'Is this still funny for you? What should I do?! Let's go to this domullo, please,' Faridun implored us.

We went with him, with Abdulvasi grumbling all the way:

'How can people believe into such nonsense? Life does not teach them anything. Faridun, have you read the classics books, or do you only believe in rumours?'

With all of his thoughts occupied with other things, though, our friend did not hear a word. Having approached the house of the "saviour," he didn't even knock on the door, but rushed into the yard through the open gate. The son of the domullo came out to meet us, and greeting us politely said:

'My father is praying now and will be out in a few minutes.'

In his conversation with the "saviour," Faridun could not hide his excitement in explaining the current situation. The domullo answered with a smile that he would pray, but everything is ultimately in the hands of Allah.

'Yet they say you can obtain a sunny day from Allah by praying. I invited many guests and the best fighters, but this event is impossible to hold in rainy weather,' Faridun begged him.

'Good. If you believe, I will pray all night and request good weather from the Almighty,' the domullo said.

I read out a parting prayer, and we hurried back.

That evening became even sadder, and Faridun looked to the sky more and more often. Abdulvasi and I wondered how naive he was, and when he stepped out Abdulvasi asked with a sigh:

'Do you remember a story with a similar plot from the book of Hussein Voiz Koshifi, our classic writer, A Thousand and One Latifas? Five centuries have passed, but people don't change. Let's see what the domullo will obtain with his earnest entreaties on our behalf.'

In the morning I woke up, looked out the window and was upset. It was not just raining, but raining cats and dogs. Abdulvasi and I hastened to Faridun. He was angry and could not hide his resentment.

'I will go now to this deceiver,' he growled. 'He has not begged the sun from Allah, but a downpour!'

'Nothing can be done about it. Since it has happened like this, it's necessary to cancel the competition. Everyone will understand. Why are you so angry?' I asked, barely able to restrain myself from giggling.

'No, let's go!' Faridun barked, not calming down at all.

Realising he could not be dissuaded, we didn't let him go alone for fear he would cause a scandal.

The domullo invited us into his house. Faridun didn't even have time to utter a resentful word before the domullo started speaking instructively, but with a wry smile:

'You won't buy anything for free, and especially you won't beg anything from the sun. It only rains without money! It is impossible to beg the sun, especially on credit; the sun shines for cash only.'

Realising that we had rushed off yesterday without leaving any money for the domullo, we were embarrassed.

Getting into the car, Faridun stubbornly muttered:

'We were right not to give money to him.'

Abdulvasi and I could not help laughing: our Faridun could not be remade. Our friend hastened to deal with the coming fighters and guests. Of course, everything had to be cancelled as it rained heavily all day long.

By the evening, Faridun was ready to laugh about the whole affair. His wife, Nasiba walked around in circles and smiled guiltily. This incident became the subject of many jokes, not just in our makhalla, but throughout Khojent.

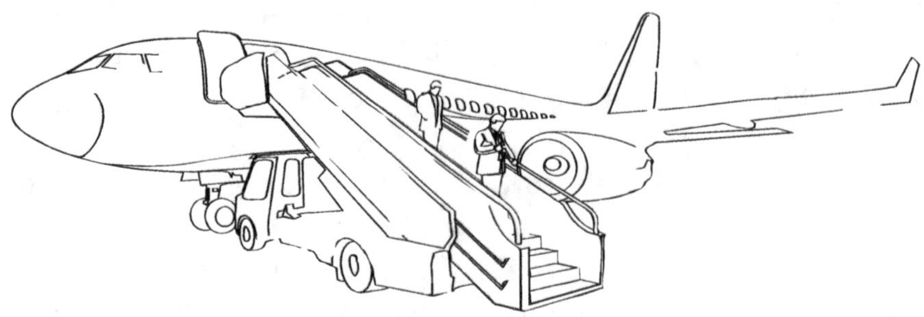

Five Minutes before Take-off

The holiday soon ended, but we had celebrated it well. We had attended the festivities surrounding the circumcision of the son of our friend, Faridun, requested the minister of the mosque to pray for the sun 'on credit,' and even sold our handsome BMW general's car. Now, we had to fly to Moscow post-haste where a new job awaited at the company belonging to the oligarch, Gleb Nikolayevich. Therefore, we decided to head to Moscow not from Khojent, but from Dushanbe.

I want to tell you more about my friend, Abdulvasi. It was him who made me and Faridun, our fellow countrymen from Navghilem, buy apartments in Khojent, the northern capital of the Republic. He assured us that over time we would save up money, sell the houses here, and settle in the capital. To Abdulvasi, there was no city in the world better than Dushanbe.

Abdulvasi was from Khojent, but had spent his student years in the capital. He studied at the Faculty of Russian Philology, and was extremely fond of literature. Abdulvasi had a habit of distorting words so that they turned out funnily. This was especially evident when talking with Russians. For example, when he uttered the word, 'sumatokha' (stramash), he pronounced it 'samatokh' (self-fuss), and the word 'speshka' (haste) turned into 'toropnya' (shaking a leg). On occasion, he declared: 'Uh, do not do samatokh and toropnya.' He also combined the two words, 'dubina' (a club) and 'duraley' (a fool) into one. The result was 'durbylyai' (twice a fool). We laughed ourselves hoarse listening to him.

Abdulvasi once told us that he was born preterm. As an important worker, his father was presented with a trip to Leningrad, and he took his pregnant wife with him. The moment they arrived, she was immediately taken to a maternity clinic. It is not for nothing that people say preterm children grow up smart, and Abdulvasi justified that saying by 200 percent. He knew Russian literature so well even our Russian friends envied him. He knew many verses by heart, and most of all he loved Pushkin and Blok.

Abdulvasi was preparing to defend his dissertation thesis covering the works of Zhukovsky, a well-known Russian poet, but the civil war which broke out in Tajikistan following the collapse of the USSR prevented this. As the head of the family, he had to change profession in order to provide the children with the things necessary for living. His wife, Malika, who was also a philologist, decided she would go to work in a kindergarten, where she registered their sons, Sheroz and Tabriz.

Abdulvasi travelled to Russia and the Baltic States, from where he moved cars to different regions. Then, to my joy, fate brought us together and we became all-weather friends. It was as if we complemented each other in everything: I proposed ideas (sometimes naïve ones), and he reasonably and calmly explained what and how to implement them, or even why we should not start that business at all. Therefore, there were no serious disputes.

The day before we left for Moscow, we flew from Khojent to Dushanbe as my friend really wanted to show me his favourite places. Before we got off the ramp, however, police officers surrounded Abdulvasi. Why? We didn't understand it, but I decided not to leave my friend.

We were bundled into a car and brought to a police station. I was not allowed into the interrogation room, but from the conversation in the car it became clear that a prisoner who looked very similar to Abdulvasi had escaped from prison in Khojent. They kept asking why his mobile phone was turned off, and my friend tried to explain that mobile phones were always switched off in an airplane, but they didn't believe him.

By the time the truth prevailed, it was gone midnight. Not having had enough sleep, in the morning we arrived at the airport. All the 'barriers' were passed, as Abdulvasi said, and we waited for the announcement for boarding. Some tired female voice announced flights in two directions very rapidly and indistinctly. We lined up at the boarding gate with our passports and tickets in hand. Peering at Abdulvasi's passport, a pretty girl asked me:

'Leningrad?' before immediately correcting herself, 'St. Petersburg?'

'Yes, Leningrad,' I answered mechanically, thinking about Abdulvasi's birthplace.

We were shepherded onto a bus, and when we reached the plane we took our seats.

'Something is wrong here,' my friend said to me anxiously.

'It's just because you can't forget the incident with the police. Calm down,' I answered.

The doors were closed, the gangway drove off, and in the cabin they announced the end of boarding for the flight to St. Petersburg.

The chaos that happened next is almost impossible to describe. Two passengers trundled up with tickets to our seats, and we showed ours to the stewardess.

'Those "impostors" need to be kicked off the plane,' I said; it seemed that we all, at some juncture, must visit police stations.

The jet bridge promptly arrived, and we were ushered onto a car that usually carried freight. In the window of the plane, the two "impostors" were shaking their fists and "saying goodbye" in the most unflattering of terms. Then we were instructed to board the correct flight. The other passengers were indignant:

'Been drunk since dawn or what?' some of them said.

'Have you overslept? It's necessary to go to bed early the night before a flight,' others added.

'So many people have been kept waiting because of you two "princes,"' others expressed their dissatisfaction.

'They boarded the wrong plane because they're hungover,' the stewardess reassured everyone.

Making our way to our seats, we passed through a hail of jeering.

'Forgive me, Abdulvasi, I'm a dunce, I don't know what came over me,' I said to my friend guiltily. 'At least we didn't fly to Novosibirsk, right?'

My friend grimaced and casually flicked me on the forehead.

'Oh, you falcon-fool!' he hissed.

'Why a 'falcon?' I asked. 'With a dunce or a dumbass, everything would be clear.'

'Because a falcon is a proud bird which flies wherever it wants,' Abdulvasi laughed amiably.

We shook hands and turned our thoughts to Moscow. What would the future hold for us there?

The Old Man, Khottabych

Abdulvasi and I flew to Moscow and immediately went to the offices of our new employer, Gleb Nikolayevich Dobrov. At the entrance to the Moscow skyscraper, tired, loaded down with luggage and in our tracksuits and well-worn sneakers, we met with an unfriendly welcome. A stout guard with a stony face looked in surprise at the outstretched business card and said in an unexpectedly squeaky voice, 'To Dobrov?'

We nodded in unison. The athletic guard introduced himself as Zabiyakin, and using an internal telephone he spoke with Gleb Nikolayevich. Then he requested we leave our luggage in the next room.

They led us through the frame of a metal detector and, having written out a pass, pointed towards the elevators. We had to go to room number 8804. Walking to the elevators, Abdulvasi nudged my side with his elbow and inquired, holding back his laughter:

'Farkhod, is not Zabiyakin an important guard, eh?'

'He is Zabiyakin! It means "badass,"' I replied.

'When Zabiyakin is silent, he is a bully, but when he opens his mouth, it's as if a goat is bleating.'

I burst out laughing:

'Well, now "Zabliyakin" (meaning fighting goat) will remain with us forever.'

I would never have known on which floor this room 8804 was, or rather I would have thought it would be on the 88th, but the building only had thirty floors. Abdulvasi suggested we go to the eighth, to which I replied:

'Well, there cannot be more than 800 rooms on one floor, can there? Come on, let's ask someone.'

'But everyone is just looking at us strangely as if we're idiots. We'd better just find him,' Abdulvasi persuaded me.

We went to the eighth floor. My friend was right: if one went to the left and in a semicircle, the numbers of rooms with one 8 began, and to the right, the rooms with two 8s were located. We only learnt that later, however. We went to Room 804, opened the doors, and there sat a young man who sneezed loudly so that it seemed to us like shots. We were dumbfounded, but he cheerfully joked:

'I'm afraid that someday the glass in the windows will shatter.'

'Or you'll give someone a heart attack,' I answered, holding a hand to my chest.

'If you're looking for Gleb Nikolayevich, then it's to the right of the elevator,' he explained, and back we went.

'Everything pulls you to the left, right?' I mocked my friend.

'And you are tempted by Leningrad instead of Moscow?' Abdulvasi said sarcastically. 'Moreover, we demanded our rights in the cabin from the real passengers, driving them away from "our" supposed places. Well, at least a stewardess figured it out five minutes before take-off and we were transferred to the correct flight.'

We headed in the opposite direction and soon found the boss's office. He spotted us immediately, since all the walls were made of glass. He smiled affably, and using the internal phone requested his secretary to let us into his office. She - strikingly beautiful and well-manicured - looked at us and asked cheerfully:

'Where are you from?'

'Down from the hall and straight from the mall. We've come directly from the plane, so do not be surprised and excuse us for the look; this is our travel clothing,' Abdulvasi answered politely.

The secretary frowned jokingly.

'Next time, I won't let you in; agreed? Here we have our own dress code.'

'A trained cat?' (words sounding almost alike in Russian) I decided to joke.

'A cat or a code, in short, it's our own uniform,' she answered with a smile. 'My name is Tamara Alekseevna,' she introduced herself, and opening the door, she let us into the chief's office.

With his eyes half-closed, Abdulvasi whispered in delight:

'Queen Tamara.'

'Tamara the Beautiful,' I answered quietly.

Gleb Nikolayevich spoke over the phone for some time before rising from his chair and inviting us to take a seat. Finally, Dobrov had some free time and came up to us with a greeting:

'Well, hello, Farkhod, hero of the classic oriental poems! Introduce me to your friend. Is he a cool driver like you?'

'Good afternoon, Gleb Nikolayevich. This is Abdulvasi; we have been working in shifts together for several years and he is a real ace in the driving seat,' I assured him.

'Well then, we'll work well together. I just don't understand how they let you in dressed in such a sports outfit. We have a routine for the working day - you will have to have a look at it,' Gleb Nikolayevich said, getting straight to the point. 'Tamara Alekseevna will show and tell you everything.'

'Do drivers here also have a white collar dress code?' Abdulvasi asked.

'Yes, the uniform is the same for everyone. I'll give you a grant to buy suits and shirts. Do you agree?' he asked.

'I do,' I answered.

We noticed how Gleb Nikolayevich watched with interest each woman passing by the glass walls of his office. The employees here were all so beautiful, slender and elegant. Abdulvasi and I shook our heads and the chief winked at us and smiled:

'At least you can look upon this beauty. A man should be satisfied by means of his eyes and appreciate the beautiful. And thus, at work, no, no! Yes, I'm now the Old man Khottabych (meaning 'would have ed'). You, young people, do not understand this.'

'Well, you don't look like an old man but a mature man in great shape,' we objected unanimously.

Abdulvasi could not resist the temptation and joked:

'Just Khottabych or Khotimych, but without age. And Gleb Nikolayevich?'

The boss laughed with satisfaction:

'Well done, Abdulvasi, you play cleverly with words. And what is your father's name? What about your education; tell me, from which high school did you graduate?'

My friend enunciated:

'Abdulvasi Abdulsalievich, Department of Russian Philology, Tajik State University.'

'Here it's customary to call everyone by their name and their father's name. It will be difficult to get used to yours, so let's call you Vasyl Salievich. Are you not against it?'

'All Russians call me Vasya.'

'Well, then Vasily Salievich, perhaps? And Farkhod, what is your father's name?' he asked, turning to me.

'Gaffar,' I answered. 'I turn out to be Farkhod Gaffarovich.'

'Fine. Tomorrow, be here at eight o'clock. Tamara Alekseevna knows the routes and addresses. Holidays and corporate parties are coming up soon and there will be a lot of work. Do you have time to buy some proper clothes? You can live in the extension of my country house. Well, that's it, the interview is over.'

We hurried out as we had much to get done before tomorrow. On the floor of the office, we carefully examined the clothes of the employees and decided to head to the nearest department store. We saw the prices of similar suits and gasped, so we took good shirts for each of us but decided to buy one suit to share. We were very different in our build, however; I was lower and denser, and Abdulvasi was taller and slimmer.

'I will turn in the length and no one will notice,' I explained busily.

'And I will look like a clown in short pants and with short sleeves? And all this will be wide on me, like on a garden scarecrow,' Abdulvasi said indignantly.

'It doesn't matter; we'll tolerate it till the first paycheck. We need to buy a lot of little things.'

'You'll be the first to start working,' my friend said earnestly. 'I'm not going to sit at the steering wheel as a clown.'

'Okay, Abdulvasi. Let's go, we need to sleep. I'll leave at seven in the morning, and you'll just put our things in their places,' I answered in a conciliatorily manner.

Dobrov's former driver had decided to go and be with his wife in Germany. He explained that by the time the chief started for work, the machine should be filled with gasoline, washed and ready to start like clockwork. Any fines from traffic cops would be deducted from our salaries.

The first day was extremely successful. I worked a lot, but I didn't feel much fatigue. Gleb Nikolayevich, despite his busy schedule, always found time to joke around and to support me. I was tormented by the thought of what would happen when the chief noticed my suit, but Gleb Nikolayevich just laughed sincerely:

'Why have you taken a suit to grow into? Hoping to catch up with Vasily Salievich? Come on, let's go to the studio and get your trousers and sleeves shortened. Be sure to change the shoes too. Remember, you are also the face of my company.'

What was I supposed to say?

When the chief saw Abdulvasi in our common suit the next day, he almost fell over he laughed so hard.

'Everything is clear! You decided to save money. No, that will not do. You'll go shopping now with Tamara Alekseevna. She will teach you how to value your image.'

My first working day was long, but I wanted to prepare the car for tomorrow for Abdulvasi. In my absence, he put both the house and the garage in order.

'Well, are you not tired?' my friend asked, coming out to meet me. As always, he could not resist a joke:

'The whole day with the steering wheel in your hands, perhaps you mixed it with a round cracknel and could not stand the temptation not to eat it?'

'About this round cracknel, do not brother; one will break all their teeth on it. And Gleb Nikolayevich will not allow us to live on a starvation diet. We are lucky with the chief, aren't we?'

'Yes, he is a good man,' Abdulvasi agreed. 'And he justifies his surname, "Dobrov" (a kind man). And the Old Man Khottabych, a wizard from an old children's film, is evidently his favourite hero. It was not for nothing that Gleb Nikolayevich jokingly renamed himself "Old man Khottabych." Let's leave this nickname for the boss just between ourselves.'

I agreed:

'"Dobrov is the Old man Khottabych." He told me he grew up in Tajikistan and made many friends there. Well, inviting us to work for his firm was also a kind of friendly deed.'

'We'll pay back Dobrov with our kindness to Dobrov,' Abdulvasi joked extemporarily.

At that moment, my phone rang.

'The Old man Khottabych has called us. Let's go to the chief!'

The First Blow is Half the Battle

'I wonder why the chief has called us at the end of the working day,' Abdulvasi said.

'Our business isn't to question but to be on time; the Old Man Khottabych does not like to wait,' I answered whilst getting into the car. 'Let's hurry!'

'Farkhod, do not ride the horses hard,' Abdulvasi said, not missing the chance to quote the words of his favourite song by Boris Shtokolov.

He immediately turned on the stereo, and a powerful bass voice started a story about a coachman and his passenger who had nowhere to rush to.

In the entrance hall, we were met by Mikhail Sergeyevich Zabiyakin, the head of the security staff. He looked critically at our jeans and white shirts, saying that we once again had not observed the dress code, and grinned:

'As a tradition we introduce new employees to the whole team. Don't worry, friends, this is just getting acquainted.'

We went up to the seventh floor conference hall, and the beautiful Tamara Alekseevna showed us to our places. Employees, it seemed, escorted newcomers with friendly smiles. Gleb Nikolayevich introduced us as the senior drivers.

'Colleagues, please love and favour the newcomers, Vasily Salievich and Farhod Gaffarovich. By the way, these are my countrymen from Tajikistan. I think we'll work well together. It will be necessary to support them and help them get used to our friendly team quickly. And I want you, dzhigits, to prove yourself to be top-class professionals.'

Suddenly, he added in Tajik:

'Miley? Do you agree?'

Surprised exclamations were heard in the hall.

'Tashakkur, thank you, Gleb Nikolayevich, we will not let you down,' we assured the boss with one voice.

The meeting ended and the employees said goodbye to us, everyone shaking our hands. We left the building together with Gleb Nikolayevich and Zabiyakin, who immediately noticed a group of migrants who were not allowed into the offices.

'It looks like they are Tajik guest workers,' Abdulvasi told the chief.

Gleb Nikolayevich approached them to find out what was the matter. It turned out they were construction workers from Tajikistan. They had been waiting for the arrival of Faridun for several days, and therefore they had sought me out as they were worried by the delay to his arrival.

'Mikhail Sergeyevich, let everyone into the entrance. Let Farkhod talk with his compatriots and Vasily Salievich will take me to my meeting and then return for his friend.'

'Just a minute, Vasily Salievich,' said Zabiyakin; 'one obligatory instruction. In case of danger, press this button,' he continued, pointing to an inconspicuous button under a control panel and fastening a name badge, "Vasily Salievich," with information about his place of work on his shirt pocket.

'Thank you, Mikhail Sergeyevich,' Abdulvasi said, and they shook hands amicably.

I went with my countrymen. It turned out they were from the brigade of our friend, Faridun, who had been delayed in Tajikistan for reasons unknown. Their employer had set a deadline: if Faridun did not appear next day, he would hire a different team.

'Where could our Faridun have disappeared to? Has he decided to hold another competition of wrestlers as a celebration devoted to circumcision of his son?'

Faridun's Moscow number was disconnected, so I dialled Khojent. He answered straight away, as if he had been expecting my call. I explained that his employer would only wait for one more day, and after that he would change the team. Faridun assured me he would be in Moscow the next day and would tell us the reason for his delay. My countrymen from the brigade thanked me and, feeling encouraged, they went home.

I stayed and waited for Abdulvasi. He was absent for a long time, and it seemed he had got stuck in a traffic jam. Suddenly, I saw Zabiyakin sprinting up to me:

'Quickly, rush to the car, Farkhod! Vasily Salievich's defence mechanism has been activated.'

I sat next to Mikhail Sergeyevich trembling. A single thought was spinning around in my head: my friend was in trouble. What would I say to his parents, wife and children?'

Without turning his head, Zabiyakin squinted one eye in my direction and said firmly:

'Calm down, Farkhod. Everything is under control.'

He turned on a surveillance camera and we saw three skinheads beating up two migrants. It seemed to that Abdulvasi recognised the Tajiks, and in a couple of seconds the skinheads would kick them to death. Abdulvasi deftly drove onto the sidewalk, dividing the combatants with the car. Leaning out of the window, he shouted, 'Run away!'

The victims instantly disappeared from the "battlefield," wiping the blood from their broken faces. Opening the car door wide on the other side, with a friendly smile Abdulvasi said to the dumbfounded skinheads:

'Do you want a ride? You are welcome!'

The trinity rushed at the car, and toying with a pistol, their leader jabbed at Abdulvasi's badge:

'Vasily Salievich? An Asian chock! Do you think you're a hero? You will have a forehead with a hole in it.'

A second thug objected contemptuously, as if spitting out his words:

'And waste a bullet on this shit? Let's throw him in the road and steal his cool car, it will come in handy for us.'

The third chipped in with his own proposal:

'We'll bury you; no one will search for you. There are a great many of you foreigners here in Moscow; you're a dime a dozen. At every turn there are Chinese, Caucasians, Uzbeks, Tajiks and Kyrgyz. We're the patriots of Russia, the orderlies of the country, and we'll kill you all.'

'Hitler also considered his race special, but what happened to him? Do not forget history,' Abdulvasi objected.

Then one of the scumbags shoved his knuckleduster into the camera, and the image disappeared.

'Don't worry, Farkhod, in twenty minutes the car will stop and the sensors will show there's no gas. We'll have to get there quickly, and the police will follow,' Mikhail Sergeyevich said.

Arriving at the scene, we slowed down, turned off the headlights, and began to inspect the area. The road went through a forest and we heard the signal on our left-hand side, so we headed in that direction.

Quietly, we got out of the car and saw such a picture. Our Abdulvasi had dug his own grave, and was reciting a poem-prayer by M.Yu. Lermontov in a sonorous voice:

When the minutes of this life are hard,
And when heart is sad,
This prayer, marvellous by heart,
I constantly have read.

There is fertile force within
The concord of live words.
The sacred charm is breathing in,
Not clear in the plots.

The burden will roll rapidly
Away, the doubt's far;
And you believe, cry happily,
And easy the days are.

(Translated by Valetine Ilyin-Pechenov)

I knew that Abdulvasi was writing a thesis on the theme, 'Poems-Prayers of the Famous Russian Poets,' but Mikhail Sergeyevich was extremely surprised.

On the other side of the grave, the three skinhead scumbags sat staring impatiently at their victim. With an elongated face and a long nose, their leader looked like Pinocchio. The second one (like a copper knob) had a face covered in freckles. Abdulvasi would definitely be calling him "Freckled" inwardly. The third had a vicious snout with long ears-locators, like Dumbo.

I shouted to my friend:

'Abdulvasi, chee hel? (how are you?)' and running up, I pulled the shovel from his hands, plotting to use it in our defence.

'Oh, oh! Another log (Paki) has come and even with a friend? Are you, man, his support group? We'll kill you together with them,' the insolent fellows scoffed.

Zabiyakin grinned and squeaked:

'Take care of your nose, "Pinocchio!"'

Our Mikhail Sergeyevich apparently did not have such a surname for nothing. He spun in place, threw up his long leg with a size 46 boot and thrust his heel right into the leader's nose. At the same time, he whacked "Freckled" with his left elbow and smashed "Dumbo" in the ribs with his right palm. So, the attackers turned into the victims.

'Who else wants a heel in his forehead?' Mikhail Sergeyevich asked.

In response, moans and curses were heard from the defeated.

I held out my hand to Zabiyakin:

'Ofarin, Mikhail Sergeyevich; that means 'well done!' Thank you for helping my friend. Where did you serve?'

'Special forces,' Zabiyakin answered.

Then the police arrived in a patrol car, and, after that, our Dobrov did. I hadn't even noticed when Zabiyakin had managed to call the boss.

The skinheads were loaded into a car and taken to a police station.

Zabiyakin approached Dobrov:

'Gleb Nikolayevich, can I take you all home? Dzhigits need to recover after such a shock.'

'Thank you, Mikhail Sergeyevich, for your service and friendship,' Dobrov answered. 'Farkhod will drive the car, and I will be a passenger with Vasily Salievich.'

Zabiyakin nodded. We got into the "cool" car, which had not become the bounty of the scum, and drove home. By inertia, I turned on the disc with Shtokolov's romantic song, "Coachman, don't ride the horses hard."

'What a great voice,' Dobrov said admiringly. 'I wish our Zabiyakin had such a bassy voice.'

I giggled out of habit, and Abdulvasi looked at the chief remorsefully:

'Gleb Nikolayevich, I'm dumb, as it turns out because I called Mikhail Sergeyevich "Zabliyakin" for his squeaky voice.'

'"Zabiyakin-Zabliyakin," Dobrov laughed. 'Well, you are too much, Vasily Salievich! Please, don't tell anyone at the office that; got it?'

'Got it,' Abdulvasi answered. 'Mikhail Sergeyevich heard me mock him, and yet today he risked his life to save me.'

'Yeah, that's it,' Dobrov agreed. 'That's the way it is in Moscow now. Well, the first blow is half the battle.'

Tsar Cauldron

As you already know from my previous stories, friends, our life turned out to be full of adventures. To be honest, Abdulvasi and I always try to dilute any trouble with a joke, but our Faridun, there is such sin inside of him he immediately falls into a panic over mere trifles. Then he begins to lament: 'How to be? You wouldn't wish such a life even on your enemy.' Abdulvasi and I have to convince our friend in practice that the world is beautiful, only we ourselves need to protect it, not destroy it.

This time, our Faridun flew to the capital after a great delay, and his Moscow employer on the construction site followed up on his threat: he fired Faridun along with the whole brigade of Tajik guest workers, and hired others. At the end of the working day, our sad friend came to the office to share his misfortune with us.

Abdulvasi and I were in a rush - we transported the foreign guests using two cars. Faridun patiently waited for us, sitting on a bench outside the office until we were finally free. Our friend looked pitiful, biting his lips and barely holding back the tears. I silently embraced him, but Abdulvasi could not help but to start the cross-examination. We knew that our Tajik brothers had lost out because of Faridun; where could we find them a job now? Faridun had let himself and the workers down.

Faridun was late arriving in Moscow because of a subpoena. In Tajikistan, we have adopted (in order to save money or what?) a law limiting financial expenditure on ritual events and the number of guests. Abdulvasi and I were present at the thuy celebrations and saw with our own eyes that Faridun had not allowed for any superfluities. I already told you that a downpour ruined the plans for a wrestling match, and the mullah didn't beg God for the sun for that day, either on credit or for cash. Nevertheless, some "vigilant" neighbour had written a denunciation of Faridun, and even provided photographs of "extra guests" - those sat on fences watching the celebration and clapping their hands, who Faridun's wife, a kind soul, had treated to sweets. That was how the interrogators made their headcount, assigning a large fine to Faridun for breaking the law.

Abdulvasi could not help reproaching:

'God sees everything: the money you wanted to spend on wrestlers went on a fine, and if the competition had taken place and twice as many people had come to look at them, eh?'

'I've got into such debt. I'm dead broke and you're joking all the time,' Faridun hissed, taking offense.

'Broke! It's a breakage of our own net; that's what it's called. Now we need to think about employing the whole team. If they leave, what will you do?' I asked.

Faridun lowered his head.

At that moment, Gleb Nikolayevich came out of the building. He looked at us and asked:

'What kind of problem are you solving? It looks like your friend and the whole brigade have been left idle? Come on; introduce me to your foreman.'

'This is our Faridun, our "slumdog millionaire." He decided to surprise everyone on the occasion of the circumcision of his son, and now he's head over ears in debt,' I answered.

'Well, hello Faridun,' Gleb Nikolayevich said, extending his hand amiably. 'I'll be waiting for you tomorrow morning, and we'll see how we can assist you. Don't let the guys from the team leave yet. Let's go, Farkhod. And you, Abdulvasi, don't leave your friend. Stay together.'

We got into the car and Gleb Nikolayevich began to ask me about Faridun, for how many years he'd been working in Moscow, what kind of construction work he'd fulfilled, and whether he had reliable guys in his team. I told him everything, and the chief suddenly replied in verse:

'The sage said with a smile on his whiskers:
"Everything is vanity and bothering.
You have a palace, a deposit, cottages,
But the flow of eternity is uncaring.'"

'I dabbled in poetry during my student years. I tried to write like the eastern sage, Mushfiki. And this is true now. We fuss a lot, losing some human qualities along the way. Here's another old verse of mine, which is appropriate to remember:

The only interchange will calculate:
Souls change: just "'give-and-take.'"

'Gleb Nikolayevich, it's very similar to our oriental poets,' I couldn't help praising the boss. 'You are a rare person and your kindness radiates upon everyone.'

'Eastern education,' Dobrov responded with a smile. 'I know these customs of yours, the men work for a whole year in order to spend everything in one day. Tomorrow we will consult on how we can help your poor compatriot.'

Dobrov told me that he was born and raised in Dushanbe, and then lived in Nurek, where his grandfather worked as the deputy head for construction of the trust, NurekGESstroy:

'Many things connect me with Tajikistan; unforgettable memories of kind and helpful people. I can't even believe that a fratricidal war could have happened in this sunny, peaceful, multi-ethnic republic.'

The next day, after talking with the chief, Faridun perked up. His team was entrusted with the construction of country houses and summer cottages for the company's employees. Meeting me, Tamara Alekseevna said with a smile:

'Oh, Gleb Nikolayevich appreciates the Tajiks. Soon, your language will be mastered in our campaign. For example, I know that the Tajik word 'zebo' means 'beautiful.'

I put my hand to my heart and bowed to our Queen Tamara, and then Zabiyakin called me:

'Farkhod, Gleb Nikolayevich said you have another New Year in the East. He wants to arrange festivities in Moscow, and he told me to to find out the details from you.'

'Mikhail Sergeyevich, let's discuss everything. According to our traditions, it is imperative to make a real pilaf in a cauldron for all the employees and guests.'

On March 21st, Navruz fell on a working day, so after consulting with the chief we postponed the holiday until the weekend. We invited the employees, their families and children for the whole day.

Abdulvasi urgently called our friends, singers and musicians without whom Navruz would not be Navruz. Tamara Alekseevna was chosen as the bride of the holiday, and she was requested to come in white clothing with an obligatory oriental crown on her head.

Faridun's construction team had a good cook, and we pledged to help him. The cook had his own forty litre cauldron for large events, which we brought from a construction site by car. Faridun decided to distinguish himself during its unloading. We were pushing the cauldron upside down from the back of the car, when suddenly Faridun, spreading his arms like wings, took hold of the side handles and decided to place it on the ground by himself. He did not calculate for its weight, however, and the cauldron fell down, covering him as the sound of the falling colossus was heard throughout the area. We were scared. People began to knock on the sides of the cauldron and call out to our friend. Moans were heard from within, so we understood that Faridun was alive. Five of us turned the cauldron over and saw our friend lying on the ground, curled up in a ball. On hearing our screams, he quietly stood up and pointed to his ears. We were glad that he wasn't badly injured, but it seemed he couldn't hear very well.

'In Moscow there are a Tsar Cannon and a Tsar Bell. A Tsar Cauldron has now appeared; yes, also there is also a Hercules-Faridun with it,' Abdulvasi could not resist joking.

'And he does not hear as the cauldron's ringing has deafened him. He needs to see a doctor,' Mikhail Sergeyevich said sternly. 'You see to the preparations, and Farkhod will accompany him to a first-aid station.'

Thank God, Faridun just had a slight contusion. Prescribing medications and eardrops, the doctor assured us his hearing would be restored in a week.

Navruz was great fun. The beautiful Tamara Alekseevna greeted everyone as the hostess of the holiday, and Gleb Nikolayevich danced to Tajik rhythms, inspiring everyone. Children ran around happily playing with each other; kids sat with their parents, and teenagers recited poetry and sang, receiving gifts from Faridun's hands. He moved aside for the musicians and rejoiced like a child, feeling like Grandfather Frost (Russian Santa Claus).

At the end of the holiday, Dobrov asked me and Abdulvasi to congratulate everyone with poems in Tajik. I read folk quatrains, and Abdulvasi read from Omar Khayyam's Rubáiyát. Gleb Nikolayevich also remembered Khayyam in Russian, and read out his poem:

'The good is always marvellous,
and it is never boisterous.
The good is warm, wholehearted,
This is its essence on the whole.

Well enough is left alone,
The good is awaited from morning till morning.
Nobody could buy the good,
Because it has one master – God.'

The holiday was a success. Our construction workers sang a well-known song from the movie, I've Met a Girl, and the guests began to sing along with great feeling.

That was how we merged into Moscow life. We gathered together again - three fellow countrymen from mountainous Tajikistan. We found good jobs, a roof over our heads, and most importantly we found kind, sympathetic friends who did not segregate people by their ethnicity.

I would like to talk about each of them in detail, with humour and anecdotes, but these will be different stories.

ФАРХОД

ИЗ НАВГИЛЕМА

ЛОНДОН
2021

СОДЕРЖАНИЕ

Юмор нам жить помогает

Гульсифат Шахиди приготовила для своих читателей и поклонников неожиданный подарок – юмористическую повесть «Фарход из Навгилема». На сей раз её герои не женщины и дети, а три неразлучных весельчака – Фарход, Абдулваси и Фаридун. Земляки из горного кишлака Навгилем твёрдо верили в себя и упорно воплощали в жизнь незатейливую мечту – получить высшее образование, построить дом и спокойно и счастливо растить детей с любимой женой.

Эти светлые планы разрушила жестокая, братоубийственная гражданская война в Таджикистане 1990–93 годов. В разорённой родной республике оказались никому не нужными дипломированные специалисты, и, чтобы прокормить семью, друзьям пришлось пополнить армию мигрантов. Фарход и Абдулваси стали перегонять машины из Германии в Россию, и их приключения в стиле «смех сквозь слёзы» описаны в рассказе «Яйца Фаберкюва». А Фаридун «прописался» на стройках Москвы и Подмосковья и полученные навыки пытался применить в благоустройстве домов друзей (рассказ «Зайчики»).

В разных жизненных ситуациях герои повести не падают духом, наоборот, щедро сдабривают разговоры и споры шутками и анекдотами. И вдали от родных мест друзей окружают хорошие люди (рассказы «За пять минут до взлёта», «Старик Хотябыч», «Лиха беда – начало!», «Царь-казан»). Фарход, Абдулваси и Фаридун умеют признавать свои ошибки, достойно выходить из неприятностей и первыми готовы посмеяться над собой (рассказы «Держи вора!», «Солнышко в кредит», «Слёт майнушек на БМВ»).

Я намеренно не раскрываю сюжеты историй, придуманных Гульсифат Шахиди, чтобы не лишить читателей новизны восприятия. И всё же не могу не дать расшифровку личного плана. Одного из героев повести Гульсифат назвала Глеб Николаевич и придумала ему фамилию Добров. Это дань памяти моему мужу – журналисту, поэту и писателю Глебу Николаевичу Дейниченко – выпускнику филологического факультета Таджикского госуниверситета. А его знаменитые слова-перевёртыши вложены в уста Фархода и Абдулваси. Я безмерно благодарна Гуле за это, ведь каждый, кто близко знал Глеба Дейниченко, снова вспомнит его, прочитав повесть и его стихи.

Новые герои Гульсифат Шахиди не очерствели сердцем в наше непростое время. Юмор помогает им скрашивать жизнь, корректировать отношения с окружающими. Я очень надеюсь, что читатели полюбят парней из Навгилема и примут их в круг своих друзей.

Вера Дейниченко,
журналистка

Познакомимся?

Меня зовут Фарход. Я обычный парень из красивого горного селения Навгилем на севере Таджикистана. По-соседству с нами жили узбеки, которые не произносили букву «ф». И поэтому всё моё детство во дворе меня звали не иначе, как Парход, а то и вовсе «пароход». Но детство прошло, я стал взрослым, и, слава Богу, все перестали коверкать моё имя. А представьте, как называли моего друга Фаридуна? Паридун, Пардон, ну и так далее. Он был шестым сыном в семье. Когда он родился, отец его пришёл навеселе и на весь двор крикнул: «От меня только сыновья!» После этого, как говорили злые языки, во всех семьях, где были одни девочки, вдруг начали рождаться похожие на соседа мальчишки.

Но давайте лучше обо мне. У нас в семье трое сыновей, и я младший – ровесник Фаридуна (это чтобы никто ничего не подумал).

История моего имени Фарход очень интересная. Мама не устаёт повторять её на все лады. Рядом с моей двоюродной бабушкой (не знаю, правильно ли так называть сестру своей бабушки?) жили соседи, у которых было одиннадцать детей. Все имена их начинались на букву «Ф». Младших детей они назвали необычными для таджиков именами – Фидель, Флора, Фрида, причём одна из старших сестёр была Фарида. Когда я родился, у нас гостила эта двоюродная бабушка. Она-то, старая и мудрая, решила назвать меня Фарходом. Объяснила маме, что в той многодетной семье больше всего ей нравился Фарход, как самый умный, добрый, хороший, вежливый среди детей. Я до сих пор задаю себе вопрос: «А если бы самым-самым был Фидель? Ох, как бы я жил с таким именем?»

Мы – дети времени бессмысленной гражданской войны 90-х годов в Таджикистане – как-то быстро повзрослели. Когда закончили школу, а потом институт, я по примеру моих ровесников подался в Россию трудовым мигрантом. Женился я рано, сразу после школы на девочке-однокласснице красавице Латофат. Это была моя первая любовь. Тогда мы решили, пока не закончим вуз, не будем заводить детей. Но, как говорится, мы предполагаем, а Бог располагает. По завершении учёбы у меня родилось уже двое детей – дочка Лайло и сын Ораз. Я понял, надо ехать на заработки, чтобы поставить их на ноги.

С детства я частенько садился за руль отцовской машины и ездил вместе с ним. Когда подрос, несмотря на запреты отца, втихаря катался сам, хотя и боялся его гнева. Как-то, давая задний ход, одним колесом влетел в арык. Пришлось звать на помощь людей. Машину вытащили, и я тихонечко прибыл на ней домой. Даже царапины не было!

На другой день отец уехал по делам, а по дороге у машины спустилось колесо. Сколько ни старался отец вытащить запасное, не мог. Оказалось, когда я влетел в арык, машину так зажало, что запасное колесо просто «приросло» к багажнику. Отец ничего не мог понять. А я-то сразу смекнул, но сделал вид, что сам удивлён. Такая практика сделала меня хорошим водителем, и в 16 лет я уже получил права в дальнем районе, переделав свою метрику на восемнадцатилетнего. Вот такой был молодой, да ранний.

Первая моя работа в качестве трудового мигранта была связана с перегоном машин из Европы в родной Таджикистан. Практика моя по вождению, как вы поняли, была богатая, поэтому со временем я стал считаться асом. Ездили мы в паре, чтобы поддерживать друг друга в дороге, и назывались сменщиками. Мой друг Абдулваси, или просто Вася, уже несколько раз перегонял машины, но только из России. Вот мы и решили поехать сами в Германию, чтобы за многие услуги не переплачивать. Ну и прогадали. А почему, поймёте сами.

Яйца Фабержюва

Не удивляйтесь, я грамотный человек и не думайте, что сделал ошибку. Речь не о знаменитом ювелире Фаберже – изготовителе пасхальных яиц, а про обычные куриные яйца. Теперь расскажу всё подробно. У меня вся жизнь не без приключений.

Первый наш выезд за границу начинался очень даже благополучно. Мы поехали в Германию. В пригороде Потсдама был пункт по сдаче старых машин, которые по мере их состояния должны идти на утилизацию. В пункте знали, что «бывшие советские» приезжают за подержанными машинами, и поэтому старались из нескольких машин одной марки собрать автомобиль почти как новый с нормальными показателями. И продавали – это было всё законно. Мы с другом выбрали одну, точно такую, как нам заказали. Оформив документы и заплатив за всё, уже через два дня мы радостные поехали назад. Ну какие же немцы пунктуальные, многим бы поучиться!

Подъезжая к границе бывшего Союза, мы уже почувствовали разницу.

В Литве, в Каунасе предстояло сделать первую растаможку. Прямо рядом с пунктом, на стоянке, к нашей радости, были места, и мы сразу поставили машину первой, не обратив внимания на то, что многие другие автомобили стояли в отдалении.

Вдруг за невысокой решёткой стоянки мы увидели небольшого роста старичка. Он нам так мило улыбался! Мы поздоровались, а он засмеялся.

Я сказал Васе, что он напоминает мне комиссара Жюва – актёра Луи де Фюнеса из французского фильма «Фантомас». Особенно его хитрая улыбка и маленькие с прищуром глазки. Старичок повернулся к нам, и мы увидели в его руках настоящую рогатку. Посмеялись. Пошли перекусить и поискать ночлег, ведь рано утром надо было возвращаться.

Радуясь, что можем первыми пройти все таможенные процедуры, мы спокойно поели и заснули. Утром ни свет ни заря побежали на таможню.

И что мы увидели? Вся машина была как будто выкрашена в грязно-жёлтый цвет и так блестела в первых лучах солнца!

Сначала мы подумали, что кто-то подменил авто. Когда подошли поближе, ужас охватил нас! По всей машине были разбиты... яйца! Да, настоящие сырые куриные яйца! А из дома напротив на нас с хитрой улыбочкой смотрел вчерашний старичок, крутя в руках ту самую рогатку...

Мы бегом к таможенникам узнать, что ж такое случилось с нашей машиной. Ответ был прост, что здесь все уже знают нашего старика-разбойника и никогда напротив его дома автомобили не ставят. Благо кур у него много и все несушки. Никакие уговоры и вызовы в полицию не помогают. У него и справка от психиатра есть.

– А что ж вы нам вчера об этом не сказали? – спросили мы.

– Ну вы же хотели первыми пройти, вот и будете теперь ждать сколько надо.

Мы со вздохом заняли очередь и по указанному таможенниками адресу поехали в специализированную мойку. Видимо, здесь работал свой подряд...

Что такое разбитое яйцо, вы, конечно, себе представляете. А когда засохли почти сто разбитых? Мыть машину самим – только покарябать, приклеившаяся скорлупа своё дело делает. Вот и пришлось потратиться на лучшую мойку, где нас встретили громким смехом. О нашем старичке, оказывается, знал весь Каунас. Я от обиды не находил себе места. Ведь так радовался, что сэкономили, а теперь потратились вдвойне, да пришлось ещё сутки ждать.

Когда уже прошли таможню, мы всё-таки остановились у домика «комиссара Жюва», чтобы узнать, за что он нас так наказал. Тот лишь улыбнулся и стал рассматривать свою рогатку, а потом сказал с хитрецой: «Зато надолго запомните дядюшку Фабера».

– Мы на всю жизнь запомним Вас, дорогой комиссар Фабержюв, – ответил я.

– Ну и хорошо, значит теперь машины будете ставить подальше от моего домика.

Дядюшка Фабер удовлетворённо раскрыл бегающие маленькие глазки и с хитрой улыбкой отвернулся. В руках за спиной он теребил ту же рогатку.

Прошло много лет, но мы с Абдулваси – Васей любим рассказывать друзьям эту историю про яйца Фабержюва. А теперь я и с вами поделился.

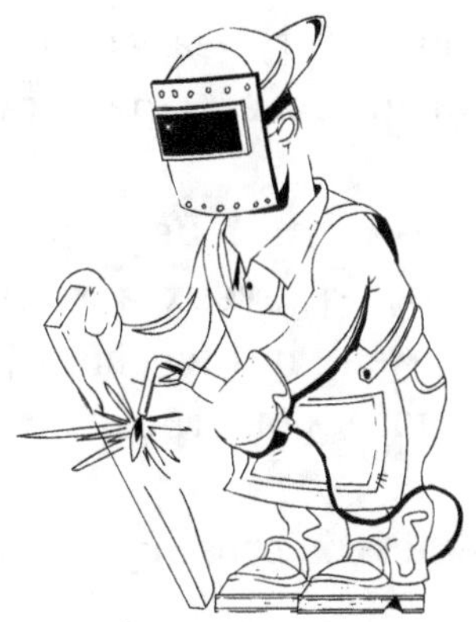

Зайчики

Через пять лет моей трудовой мигрантской деятельности (а как звучит!) я скопил немного денег и купил на окраине Ходжента старенькую трёхкомнатную квартиру в кирпичном доме. Жили там раньше немцы, которые уехали от нашей гражданской войны подальше. Квартира была – просто загляденье! Немцев за аккуратность и хозяйственность можно только похвалить. Я был очень рад, что поселился в микрорайоне рядом с моими друзьями Фаридуном и Абдулваси. Единственный недостаток в квартире – первый этаж и нет решёток. Годы были неспокойные, и я перед очередным отъездом решил окна загородить.

Поспрашивал у друзей, где найти хорошего мастера.

– Э-э-э, не переживай, – сказал Фаридун, – сами что-нибудь придумаем.

Он-то в этом разбирался, работал на стройке в Подмосковье.

– Вон там, на заброшенной стройке, много арматуры оставили, – добавил предприимчивый Абдулваси. – Заберём, всё равно бесхозная лежит.

– А как же дальше? – спросил я.

– Спросим у кого-нибудь, покажут! Неужели мы, три мужика, не сделаем? – заверил Фаридун. – Во-первых, нужна арматура, а она прямо под носом валяется. Во-вторых, нужен газовый баллон и сварочный аппарат. В-третьих, нужен эскиз, вернее чертёж, ну в общем рисунок.

– Сразу видно политехнический институт заканчивал, всё бы тебе чертежи чертить, – перебил его Абдулваси. – Решётки, они и есть решётки, не в театре же будем ставить, э-э-э.

– Пусть не в театре, но и не в тюрьме же! – не унимался Фаридун.

– Слушайте, во-первых, во-вторых, в-третьих, в театре, в тюрьме – надоели! На руках билеты, завтра летим в Москву. Времени нет на споры, – остановил их я.

– Фарход, тогда из картона вырежи – и быстро, и без проблем, – обиженным голосом проговорил Фаридун.

Решили, что мы с Абдулваси пойдём на стройку за арматурой, а Фаридун – добывать остальное.

На заброшенной стройке было тихо. Мы подошли к куче строительного материала. Стали нагружать тележку арматурой и тут же прикинули, сколько понадобится её на два окна и большую веранду. Закончили погрузку и решили идти назад. Но не тут-то было! Перед нами как будто вырос сторож – большой пёс. Он вроде миролюбиво вилял хвостом. Мы решили обойти его, а он не пропускает. Что делать? Оказывается, хозяева стройки бросили всё, и даже собаку. Теперь понятно стало, почему стройматериалы никто не трогал.

Я позвонил Фаридуну (да здравствуют мобильники!), всё объяснил и попросил купить ливерной колбасы, у моей жены взять снотворные таблетки и быстрее к нам. Латофат ничего не поняла, но, зная мои чудачества, отдала таблетки.

Фаридун прибежал и покормил пса. Тот с удовольствием съел колбасу и стал засыпать. Мы оставили Фаридуна с ним, а сами с тяжёлым грузом поспешили к дому. Фаридун вдогонку крикнул, что привёл мастера и тот ждёт со своей техникой.

Мы узнали, что было со «сторожем» только через час. Оказывается, снотворное подействовало на псину всего лишь на 14 минут. Потом Фаридун стал его отвлекать и взобрался на дерево. Нет, собака его не тронула. Пришли ребятишки, стали подкармливать пса, и он пошёл за ними. А Фаридун от страха на дерево-то высоко залез, а спуститься не мог и упал, ударившись об ветки. Ободрался весь с головы до ног! Ему-то ещё повезло, а вот что с нами было? Послушайте!

Мы с Абдулваси не стали ждать Фаридуна, поговорили со сварщиком и начали работу. Сварщик сделал каркасы, а мы стояли рядом и «сочиняли» орнамент для окон поскромнее. Загудел сварочный аппарат, искры во все стороны, а мы глядели и не понимали, зачем мастеру такие огромные солнцезащитные очки. Решётки для окон мы сразу прибили на место.

Для веранды работы оказалось вдвое больше. Мне хотелось чего-то необычного. Но, увы, я не художник. А сварщику что, мы говорим – он делает. Да постоянно просит стоять нас подальше. Нам даже обидно стало, вроде как от себя отгоняет. Через час мы уже забивали большую решётку на веранду.

В это время подошёл ободранный и покорябанный Фаридун. Мы так и покатились со смеху! А он, вглядываясь в наши глаза, тревожно спросил:

– Вы что, без защитных очков смотрели на сварку? Вот дураки! Вы же «зайчиков» столько наловили, что в Москве будете только через две недели! – Он махнул на нас рукой и ушёл замазывать свои раны.

Мы про «зайчиков» ничего не поняли. Расплатились со сварщиком и решили отдохнуть перед завтрашним вылетом в Москву. Работа ждёт трудовых мигрантов!

Что было потом, не описать словами. Ночью глаза опухли, даже открыть их было невозможно. Вызвали машину скорой помощи. Меня увезли в глазное отделение, где меня уже ждал мой напарник Абдулваси.

Билеты наши жёны сдали. Неделю мы лежали в больнице, ещё неделю лечились в поликлинике. Окулист – наш лечащий врач, всё подшучивал: «Ну как, хотите ещё наловить «зайчиков»?»

...А решётка на моей веранде оказалась с таким «рисунком», что через неё в некоторых местах спокойно мог пролезть не только ребёнок, но и взрослый человек. К чему же такие жертвы были, ведь мы чуть глаз не лишились?!

Теперь я знаю, что такое сварка. Лучше бы мы с Абдулваси на стройке работали, как Фаридун, а не машины гоняли.

Вот такая история с «зайчиками».

Держи вора!

Перегоняли мы с Абдулваси машины из Германии в Россию, перегоняли, да и решили приобрести одну для себя. Подумали, оформимся в московском таксопарке и займёмся посменно извозом. Продавец в Германии за время нашего «бизнеса» проникся к нам расположением и собрал очень яркую, красивую, почти как новую машину. Для нашего такси – просто класс!

Без очереди и препятствий мы получили работу, ведь документы наши и водительский стаж были в полном порядке. А может быть, и наш сияющий БМВ понравился?

Как-то я подвозил из аэропорта Шереметьево олигарха, не дождавшегося свою машину из пробок. А он спешил на ответственную встречу. Довёз я своего пассажира быстро и вовремя. Тот остался очень доволен и попросил мою визитку, отметив, что ему такие водители нужны.

Выходя из машины, он скинул плащ, и я увидел на нём рубашку точь-в-точь как у моего дяди Тахира. Такую синюю в белую крапинку я видел всего один раз – двадцать лет назад, когда подростком приезжал в Душанбе.

Мой дядя, известный и талантливый журналист, слыл модником. Ну работа у него такая – ответственные мероприятия, встречи, интервью и так далее. Мой отец и дядя были не похожи друг на друга во всём, будто из разных семей. Отец своего брата называл эстетом. Я долго не понимал почему, пока не увидел всё своими глазами.

Как-то дядя Тахир поехал в Испанию по линии Общества дружбы с зарубежными странами, но за свой счёт. В это время я гостил у них на зимних каникулах. Мы с тётей Саодат и моим двоюродным братом Тимуром с удовольствием гуляли по предновогоднему Душанбе, сияющему разноцветными огнями. Школьные каникулы в тот военный 1991 год продлили на целый месяц.

Десять дней пролетели быстро. Дядя Тахир приехал очень довольный. Мы все ждали гостинцы. Он подарил мне набор открыток с видами Барселоны, а Тимуру – сувенир из прозрачного стекла с видом столицы – Мадрида. Когда сувенир переворачивали, шёл снег, а крошечные фигурки людей так и оставались в летней одежде. Не помню, что подарил дядя Тахир жене Саодат, но он с большим удовольствием показывал целых пятнадцать мужских рубашек, которые приобрёл для себя. И всё повторял: «Здесь таких ни у кого нет!» Глаза его при этом блестели гордостью и восторгом.

А рубашки были и правда бесподобные. В те годы тотального дефицита ничего подобного достать было просто невозможно. Сорочки одна лучше другой: цветная с белым воротничком, синяя в крапинку, а ещё были в полосочку, в горошек, с рюшами, всех не перечислить. Никогда таких не видел. Но недолго дяде пришлось ими любоваться. А дальше случилось вот что.

Дядя Тахир ради форса каждый день менял свои испанские рубашки. Снимет одну, повесит на стул, вроде как расстаться даже на время стирки не мог. Наденет новую – и на работу! Только на пятнадцатый день жену попросил постирать их вручную. Тётя Саодат аккуратненько всё исполнила и хотела высушить их на веранде, поскольку накануне шёл снег, а утром от тёплого солнышка всё растаяло и потекло с крыш и деревьев.

Но дядя Тахир всё-таки решил вывесить предметы своей гордости на улицу на свежий воздух. Сам привязал бельевую верёвку подальше от капели и развесил все пятнадцать рубашек – одна лучше другой!

Сколько тётя его не отговаривала от этого, ведь могут украсть, но дядя её как будто не слышал. Сел в своём кабинете у окна и стал писать очередное интервью, одновременно наблюдая за своими рубашками.

Тётя на кухне готовила обед, а мы с Тимуром сражались в шашки в детской. Минут через пятнадцать мы услышали, как дядя с руганью выскочил из своего кабинета и вмиг очутился на улице. Мы кинулись за ним, вслед за нами прибежала испуганная тётя Саодат.

– Что случилось?! Почему?.. – и обомлела. Бельевая верёвка была пуста.

– Представляешь, какие-то сволочи за пятнадцать минут спёрли пятнадцать рубашек, – впервые от моего галантного дяди-эстета я услышал такие слова.

– А ведь я предупреждала! – с укором посмотрела тётя в нашу сторону.

Дядя расстроенно махнул рукой и весь вечер молчал, тяжело вздыхая. Недолго ему пришлось носить испанские рубашки. Но это не конец истории.

Через три дня дядя вернулся из редакции радостный.

– Представляете, я нашёл вора! – весело сообщил он нам. – Зашёл в магазин за хлебом, а прямо передо мной парень в моей рубашке! Я остановил его и спросил, откуда у него эта вещь. Парень испугался.

– Ты знаешь, кто я? – спросил дядя у воришки. – Я – известный журналист, меня знает вся республика. Все рубашки у тебя?

– Да, извините меня! Но я всё верну, – виновато ответил тот.

Дядя Тахир спросил вора, сколько времени тому понадобится, чтобы вернуть рубашки? Парень заверил, что через пятнадцать минут он будет у подъезда дома.

– Тимур, Фарход, идёмте со мной, вместе подождём на скамейке, – пригласил нас дядя.

– Кто ж так вора ловит? И ты ему поверил? Надо было сразу за шкирку и в милицию. Снял бы с него рубашку и как доказательство представил правоохранительным органам. Ты хоть спросил, как его зовут, где живёт?! Нет? Теперь ищи – свищи! Он сбежал, и след его простыл, – рассмеялась тётя Саодат.

– Как ты плохо о людях думаешь? – наивно укорил её дядя.

– Людям я верю, а ворам нет! – обиженно ответила жена. – Он тебя обокрал, обманул и радуется, что так легко отделался. Теперь сидите и ждите, пока рак на горе свистнет. Может тогда и вернутся все рубашки.

Простояли мы у подъезда почти два часа. Стало совсем темно и холодно. Дядя Тахир всё смотрел в сторону магазина, где он поймал вора. Потом тётя не выдержала и просто загнала нас домой. Рассмешила тем, что ожидание может продлиться много лет, а то и всю жизнь. А вора назвала милым, ведь он извинился за кражу.

Но дядя грустил весь вечер. Зато теперь он вспоминает то происшествие и рассказывает друзьям, как анекдот, и от души смеётся со всеми вместе. Иногда я думаю, что чудачествами и доверчивостью я очень похож на дядю Тахира.

А когда мы встречаемся с тётей Саодат, на мой вопрос, как дела, она весело отвечает:

– Всё очень хорошо, только вот ждём нашего вора с испанскими рубашками. Хотя, наверное, он уже износил их.

Знаете, о чём я подумал, глядя в своём такси на олигарха в испанской рубашке? Не он ли с подельниками умыкнул тогда с верёвки любимые дядины сорочки, а?

Слёт майнушек на БМВ

Помните, друзья, я рассказывал вам об олигархе, которого подвозил из аэропорта? Ну, я ещё увидел на нём испанскую рубашку точь-в-точь как у моего дяди Тахира? Дядины пятнадцать рубашек украли прямо с бельевой верёвки на улице, и я потом подумал на своего пассажира-олигарха, не он ли в этом участвовал. Спросить его прямо – у меня духу не хватило. Тем более, я своему пассажиру понравился, и мы даже обменялись визитками на всякий случай.

Он назвался Глебом Николаевичем. Не поверите, но олигарх позвонил мне и предложил работу водителем у него в компании. Спросил, смогу ли я найти сменщика? Вот так случай! А нам с Абдулваси позарез надо было что-то менять в жизни.

Дело в том, что друг Фаридун пригласил нас в Ходжент на туй – обрезание своего малыша. Он просил нас приехать на БМВ, ведь это как «генеральская» машина. Надо же всему народу показать, на какой машине он приедет в ресторан! Смешно? Нам-то точно смешно, а для него это было важно. Он даже мечтал купить у нас эту машину.

Мы с Абдулваси хотели поддержать нашего любимого друга, но из-за поездки на туй могли остаться без работы. И тут как раз появляется Глеб Николаевич с завидным предложением.

Я от неожиданности дар речи потерял. Но нельзя было показывать свои чувства. Сказал, что предложение интересное и я подумаю.

– Даю тебе срок две недели, – подытожил Глеб Николаевич.

– Хорошо, – сдержанно согласился я, хотя от радости готов был прыгать до потолка. Ведь сколько проблем можно было сразу решить: и поехать на торжества к другу, и продать там машину, и, главное, получить хорошую работу.

После разговора с Глебом Николаевичем мы написали заявления об уходе. Нас сразу отпустили, так как желающих водителей было много. Рано утром мы уже были в пути. Через четыре дня нас радостно встречали родные и особенно счастливый Фаридун.

Перед торжествами, как и принято в таких случаях, надо было провести много традиционных мероприятий – и утренний плов, и приход старейшин махалли для благословения обряда, и многое другое. Про женские обрядовые посиделки я должен был бы новую историю рассказать, тем более там вообще дел без конца и края. Поэтому умолчу.

... После такой дальней дороги мы решили отвезти машину на мойку, ведь рано утром предстояло ехать на утренний плов. Как же она умытая засверкала и стала ещё краше! Мы оставили машину под большим ветвистым деревом во дворе и ушли отдыхать. Спал я беспокойно, просыпаясь от неугомонного галдежа птичек майна – так у нас называют азиатских скворцов.

– Сегодня у майнушек, наверное, какое-то торжество или слёт передовиков производства, – сказал я жене. Она рассмеялась, а я опять заснул.

Что было утром? Ни свет ни заря меня разбудил Абдулваси. Он всё говорил и говорил про машину. Я спросонья ничего толком понять не мог.

– Там такая картина, не знаешь то ли смеяться, то ли плакать, – с выпученными глазами объяснял мне друг.

Я перепугался и спросил:

– Что?! Ограбили? Сняли колеса? Разбили стёкла?

– Спускайся вниз, сам увидишь, даже говорить неприятно, – буркнул Абдулваси.

Я быстро умылся, оделся и побежал к машине. Что же я увидел?! Наш красавец БМВ весь был запачкан помётом майнушек. Никакому дядюшке Фаберу из Каунаса с его рогаткой такое бы и не приснилось. Но там была чужая территория, а здесь родной

Ходжент. Мало того что машина была жуткого цвета, да ещё и запах! К ней не то что подойти близко, но даже стоять в отдалении было невозможно. Молва донесла всё до Фаридуна, и он, запыхавшись, прибежал к нам.

– Сейчас на оши нахор – утренний плов начнут гости приходить! Я хотел несколько стариков на этой машине привезти. Что же делать? – в отчаянии спросил хозяин торжества.

– Бери другую машину. Ничего не поделаешь: на этих майнушек не пожалуешься, не поругаешь их, не заставишь всё вымыть. Так что начинай свои торжества без нас. А мы на мойку! Ну что тут сказать? Наши майнушки тоже облюбовали и «обмыли» такую красивую машину на своих «торжествах», – ответил я.

Да, я забыл вам сказать, что мой друг Абдулваси умел очень смешно коверкать слова и на таджикском, и на русском. Да ещё ухитрялся перемешивать их в разговоре. Вот и на этот раз друг сдвинул набок тюбетейку и хмыкнул:

– Не обмыли машину майнушки, а наибарот! На них напал богатырь по имени Усрак! – Мы так и покатились со смеху.

Как мы сели в машину, как доехали под свист и хохот мальчишек, просто не описать. А сколько смеха было на мойке?! Работники даже за тройную цену не хотели мыть наш БМВ, но потом сжалились и попросили прийти через час.

На утренний плов пришлось идти пешком. Нас встречали как героев латифа – юмористического рассказа. Оказывается, все уже знали об этом случае и рассказывали, как анекдот, добавляя смешные подробности. Кто говорил, что мы сладкие подарки везли и птички переели. Другие уверяли, мы это сделали сами, чтобы не сглазили нашу «генеральскую» машину. Третьи твердили про происки завистников. Утренний плов был очень весёлый, смех звучал на всю махаллю – микрорайон. Мы с Абдулваси тоже смеялись, хотя утром впору плакать было.

Через час мы пошли на мойку и забрали нашу сверкающую машину.

Мы вернулись на туй, и все гости вышли посмотреть на «генеральскую» машину. И тут же один за другим стали подтрунивать:

– Ну что? Привезли машину председателя слёта майнушек?

– Ну, конечно, такую машину грех не отметить!

– Фаридун, теперь у тебя будет самая знаменитая машина! Про неё легенды впору складывать.

– Не ставь её под деревом – это актовый зал для слёта майнушек!

А дети со всей махалли не отходили от БМВ и просили их покатать:

– Поехали на слёт майнушек! Сегодня ночью у них будет праздничный концерт с ужином!

В ресторан мы поехали все вместе. За рулём гордо сидел новый владелец машины Фаридун. Сбылась его мечта! Правда, знакомые и соседи частенько с улыбкой интересовались:

– Не та ли это «генеральская» машина, которую «обмыли» майнушки?

Солнышко в кредит

Наша поездка в Ходжент на туй оказалась очень весёлой.

Друг Фаридун после обрезания сына решил удивить всех и в дни торжеств запланировал гуштингири – состязание борцов. Позвал именитых пахлавонов-богатырей нашей махалли и других микрорайонов города. Но мы предполагаем, а Бог располагает…

Вечером накануне дня состязания погода стала резко меняться. Хмурые тучи обволокли небо. Фаридун запереживал:

– Если завтра будет дождь, всё придётся отменить. Поблизости спортивного зала нет, да и с тем заранее необходимо было договариваться.

– Да распогодится, не переживай, – стал я успокаивать друга.

– Закажем пушки для разгона туч, – пошутил Абдулваси.

– Вам бы шутки шутить? А я за всё заплатил! И участников разочаровывать не хочется. Сам Султан-богатырь обещал прийти, и люди хотят посмотреть на него, – с отчаянием продолжал Фаридун.

– Ну, если он настоящий борец, ему ни снег, ни дождь не помешает, – сказал я.

– Он-то наверняка придёт, а кто смотреть будет? Под дождём даже стоять не очень-то приятно, а уж в грязи соревноваться борцам-пахлавонам – это круто! – подливал масло в огонь Абдулваси.

– Ну ладно. Как говорится, утро вечера мудренее. Будем надеяться на хорошую погоду, – печально глядя на небо, произнёс Фаридун.

И мы собрались расходиться по домам. Но к нам навстречу бежала Насиба, жена Фаридуна. Запыхавшись, она сказала, что на женских посиделках одна соседка поделилась новостью, что в соседнем микрорайоне живёт домулло Хайрулло, который может вымолить у Бога хорошую погоду. Мы с Абдулваси так рассмеялись, что нас было слышно, наверное, во всей махалле. А Фаридун с надеждой спросил жену:

– Ты узнала, где он живёт? Спросила его адрес?

Мы переглянулись с Абдулваси и опять прыснули от смеха.

– Вам всё смешно? А мне что делать?! Поедем к этому домулло, прошу вас! – умоляюще посмотрел на нас Фаридун.

Мы махнули рукой и поехали с ним. Абдулваси всю дорогу бурчал:

– Как люди могут верить такой ерунде? Ничему жизнь их не учит. Фаридун, ты книги классиков читал или только слухам веришь?

Но друг никого и ничего не слышал. Все его мысли были заняты другим. Подъехав к дому «спасителя», он, даже не постучав, рванул во двор, благо калитка была открыта. Навстречу вышел сын домулло и, вежливо поздоровавшись, сказал:

– Отец сейчас молится и через несколько минут выйдет.

В беседе со «спасителем» Фаридун никак не мог скрыть своё волнение, объясняя сложившуюся ситуацию. Домулло с улыбкой ответил, что молиться будет, но всё в руках Аллаха.

– Все же говорят, вы можете вымолить у Аллаха солнечный день! Я позвал много гостей и лучших борцов, но под дождём это мероприятие провести невозможно, – умолял его Фаридун.

– Хорошо. Если вы поверили, я буду молиться и просить Всевышнего всю ночь, – сказал служитель мечети. Прочитал напутственную молитву, и мы поспешили назад.

Вечер стал ещё более мрачным, и Фаридун всё чаще глядел на небо. Мы с Абдулваси удивлялись, какой же он наивный. Когда друг уехал, оставив нас у дома, Абдулваси со вздохом спросил:

– А ты помнишь рассказ с похожим сюжетом из книги нашего классика Хусейна Воиза Кошифи «Тысяча и одна латифа»? Уже пять веков прошло, а люди не меняются. Посмотрим, что нам намолит домулло!

Утром я проснулся, посмотрел в окно и расстроился. Шёл не просто дождик, а ливень!

Мы с Абдулваси поспешили к Фаридуну. Тот ходил злой и не скрывал обиды.

– Я поеду сейчас к этому обманщику! Он у Аллаха вымолил не солнце, а ливень. А зачем обещал?!

– Ничего, раз уж так случилось, надо отменить соревнования. Все поймут. Что ты так злишься? – спросил я, еле сдерживаясь от смеха.

– Нет, поедем! – не успокаивался Фаридун.

Мы поняли, что его не переубедить, но одного не отпустили, боясь, что он устроит там скандал.

Домулло пригласил нас в дом. Фаридун не успел и слово вымолвить, как тот с лукавой улыбкой, но поучительно заговорил:

– Бесплатно ничего не купишь, тем более не заставишь вымолить солнце. Без денег только дождь! А солнце даже в кредит невозможно выпросить. Только за наличные!

Мы смутились, вспомнив, что вчера в спешке денег домулло не оставили.

Уже садясь в машину, обиженный Фаридун упрямо буркнул нам:

– Правильно сделали, что не дали ему денег!

Мы с Абдулваси не могли сдержать смеха: нашего Фаридуна не переделаешь. Друг поспешил разбираться с пришедшими борцами и гостями. Конечно же, всё отменили, так как сильный дождь шёл весь день.

А к вечеру Фаридун смеялся уже вместе с нами. Жена его Насиба ходила кругами и виновато улыбалась. Этот случай тоже стал поводом для весёлых шуток не только в нашей махалле, но и во всём Ходженте.

За пять минут до взлёта

Праздники закончились, и погуляли мы хорошо. Были на торжествах – обрезании сынишки нашего друга Фаридуна, просили домулло вымолить солнышко в кредит, да ещё продали наш красавец БМВ как «генеральскую» машину. Теперь надо было срочно лететь в Москву – там нас ждала новая работа у знакомого олигарха Глеба Николаевича. Добираться до Москвы мы решили не из Ходжента, а из аэропорта Душанбе.

Хочу подробнее рассказать о моём друге Абдулваси. Это он нас с Фаридуном – земляков из Навгилема заставил купить квартиры в Ходженте – северной столице республики. Уверял, что со временем накопим мы денег, продадим здесь жильё и поселимся в столице. Надо сказать, что для Абдулваси лучше города, чем Душанбе, в мире не было.

Сам он был из Ходжента, а студенческие годы провёл в столице. Учился на факультете русской филологии и очень любил литературу. У Абдулваси была привычка коверкать слова так, что получалось очень смешно. Особенно это проявлялось, когда он общался с русскими. Например, слово «суматоха» он произносил «саматох», а слово «спешка» превратил в «тарапню». При случае он заявлял: «Э, не надо делать саматох и тарапня»!

А ещё он объединил два слова – «дубина» и «дуралей» в одно. Получился «дурбыляй». Мы смеялись до коликов в животе, слыша это в свой адрес.

Абдулваси как-то рассказал нам, что родился семимесячным. Отцу, как передовику производства, дали путёвку в Ленинград, он взял с собой беременную супругу. Не успели они прилететь, как жену тут же в роддом повезли. В народе не зря говорят, что такие дети вырастают умными. А Абдулваси оправдал это на все двести процентов.

Литературу русскую он знал так хорошо, что ему завидовали даже наши русские друзья. Стихов наизусть помнил множество. А больше всех любил Пушкина и Блока.

Абдулваси готовился защитить диссертацию по творчеству Жуковского, но помешала гражданская война, разразившаяся в Таджикистане после развала СССР. Пришлось ему как главе семьи сменить профессию, чтобы обеспечить детей самым необходимым. С женой Маликой – тоже филологом решили так: она идёт работать в детский сад, куда они определили своих сыновей-погодков Шероза и Табриза.

Абдулваси ездил в Россию и Прибалтику – перегонял машины. А потом, к моей радости, судьба свела нас. И в рейсы мы отправлялись вместе, о чём я вам вкратце уже рассказал.

Подружились мы накрепко. Во всём друг друга будто дополняли: я предлагаю идеи (иногда и наивные), а он аргументированно и спокойно объясняет мне, что и как надо осуществить или вообще не браться за дело. Поэтому и споров особо у нас не было.

В Душанбе мы с Абдулваси прилетели из Ходжента за день до московского авиарейса. Уж очень друг хотел показать мне свои любимые места.

Но не успели мы сойти с трапа, как Абдулваси окружили сотрудники милиции. За что? Почему? Мы не поняли, но я решил не оставлять друга. Нас посадили в машину и привезли в отделение. Меня в комнату допросов не пустили, но по разговорам в машине стало понятно, что из ходжентской тюрьмы сбежал заключённый, очень похожий на Абдулваси. И ещё его всё время спрашивали, почему у него был выключен мобильный телефон? Друг пытался объяснить, что в самолёте всегда выключает мобильник, но ему не верили.

В общем, пока дошли до истины, уже было за полночь. Вот и погуляли мы под конвоем...

Утром, не выспавшись, приехали в аэропорт. Прошли все «шлагбаумы», как говорил

Абдулваси, и стали ждать объявления на посадку. Измученный женский голос очень быстро и невнятно объявил о рейсах по двум направлениям. Мы встали в очередь к выходу на посадку. Паспорта и билеты были у меня. Симпатичная девушка спросила меня, взглянув на паспорт Абдулваси:

– Ленинград? – и тут же поправилась. – Санкт-Петербург?

– Да, Ленинград, – машинально ответил я, думая о месте рождения Абдулваси.

Нас пригласили в автобус, и мы, доехав до стоянки лайнера, сели на свои места.

– Что-то здесь не то, – тревожно сказал мне друг.

– Это ты всё не можешь забыть друзей-милиционеров. Успокойся, – ответил я.

Уже закрыли двери, отъехал трап, и в салоне объявили об окончании посадки на самолёт, вылетающий в город Санкт-Петербург...

Что было с нами, просто невозможно описать! Да ещё приходили пассажиры с билетами на наши места, а мы предъявляли стюардессе свои. Тех «самозванцев» высадили из самолёта. Такое впечатление, что все мы скопом по разным подозрениям побывали в отделении милиции.

Оперативно подъехал трап, нас посадили на машину, которая возит, цепляя, грузовые вагончики на колёсах. Навстречу нам мчалась точно такая же машина, в которой сидели двое «самозванцев», из-за нас покинувших самолёт. Они размахивали кулаками и нелестными словами «прощались» с нами. На трап московского лайнера мы вбежали за пять минут до взлёта. Пассажиры возмущались:

– Пьяные с утра, что ли? – спрашивали одни.

– Проспали, да? Ночью раньше надо было ложиться, – добавляли другие.

– Столько народу ждали двух «принцев», что блатные, да? – выражали недовольство третьи.

– Это они с похмелья ошиблись самолётом, – успокоила всех стюардесса.

Пока мы сели на свои места, прошли через шквал насмешек.

– Абдулваси, прости меня, балбеса, не знаю, что на меня нашло, – виновато сказал я другу. – Хорошо хоть не в Новосибирск улетели, да?

Мой обиженный друг сделал зверское лицо и, небольно щёлкнув меня по лбу, прошипел:

– Эх ты, сокол-балабес!

Я удивился, почему сокол? С балбесом-балабесом всё ясно.

– Потому что сокол – птица гордая, куда хочет, туда и летит, – ответил он и дружески засмеялся.

Мы пожали друг другу руки и устремили свои мысли в Москву. Что ждёт нас там?

Старик Хотябыч

Прилетели мы с Абдулваси в Москву и сразу поехали в офис к нашему новому работодателю Глебу Николаевичу Доброву. На проходной высотки Москва-Сити нас, уставших и нагруженных багажными сумками, встретили неприветливо. Дорожный прикид «а-ля Рамзан» – спортивные костюмы и видавшие виды кроссовки – не вызывал доверия. Богатырь с каменным лицом удивлённо посмотрел на протянутую визитку и уточнил неожиданно писклявым голосом: «К Доброву?».

Мы дружно закивали. По внутреннему телефону богатырь назвал себя Забиякиным и переговорил с Глебом Николаевичем. Потом попросил оставить наш багаж в соседней комнате.

Нас пропустили через рамку металлоискателя и, выписав пропуск, указали на лифты. Предстояло пройти в кабинет номер 8804.

Проходя к лифтам, Абдулваси ткнул меня локтем в бок и, сдерживая смех, спросил:

– Фарход, какой важный охранник Заблиякин, а?

– Он же Забиякин! Значит задира, – возразил я.

– Пока молчит Забиякин, а как откроет рот, точно барашек бе-е-бе-е блеет.

Я прыснул со смеху:

– Ну теперь навсегда охранник для нас Заблиякиным останется!

Я бы в жизни не понял, на каком этаже этот кабинет 8804. Вернее, подумал бы, что на 88-м. Но здание было в тридцать этажей. Абдулваси предложил поехать на восьмой, на что я ответил:

– Ну не может же быть на одном этаже более 800 кабинетов? Пойдём спросим у кого-нибудь?

– И так на нас странно все смотрят, как на придурков. Найдём мы его, – уверил меня Абдулваси.

Мы поехали на восьмой этаж. Друг оказался прав: там, если налево и по полукругу, то начинались номера кабинетов с одной восьмёрки, а направо – с двух восьмёрок. Но узнали мы об этом позже. Пошли в 804-й кабинет, открыли двери, а там сидел молодой человек и чихал так, что нам это показалось выстрелами. Мы оторопели, а он весело сказал:

– Боюсь, когда-нибудь стёкла в окнах вдребезги разлетятся.

– Или с кем-нибудь инфаркт случится, – ответил я, держась за сердце.

– Если вам к Глебу Николаевичу, то это правое крыло от лифта, – объяснил он дорогу. И мы пошли назад.

– Всё тебя налево тянет, да? – решил я подшутить над другом.

– А тебя вместо Москвы в Ленинград-Петербург?! – съязвил Абдулваси. Он намекал на то, что по моей вине на посадке в аэропорту Душанбе мы перепутали самолёт. Да ещё права качали в салоне перед пассажирами, сгоняя их с якобы «наших» мест. Хорошо хоть за пять минут до взлёта стюардесса разобралась, и нас пересадили с питерского рейса на московский.

Мы пошли в обратном направлении и скоро нашли кабинет шефа. Он нас сразу увидел, так как все стены кабинета были из стекла. Приветливо улыбнулся и по внутренней связи попросил секретаршу пропустить к себе в кабинет. Она (ну очень красивая и ухоженная!) посмотрела на нас и весело спросила:

– Откуда вы такие?

– С корабля на бал. Прямо с самолёта! Не удивляйтесь и извините нас за внешний вид. Это наша дорожная одежда, – очень вежливо ответил Абдулваси.

Секретарша шутливо нахмурила брови:

– В следующий раз не пущу! Договорились? Здесь у нас свой дресс-код.

– Дрессированный кот? – решил пошутить я.

– Кот или код, короче, своя форма одежды, – с улыбкой ответила она. – Меня зовут Тамара Алексеевна, – и, открыв дверь, она пропустила нас в кабинет шефа.

Абдулваси закатил глаза и прошептал восхищённо:

– Царица Тамара!

– Тамара Прекрасная, – также тихо подтвердил я.

Глеб Николаевич говорил по телефону и, приподнявшись со своего места, показал нам на стулья. Мы сели. Наконец Добров освободился и пошёл к нам с приветствием:

– Ну, здравствуй герой классических восточных поэм Фарход! Давай познакомь меня со своим другом. Он такой же классный водитель, как и ты?

– Добрый день, Глеб Николаевич! Это Абдулваси – мы уже несколько лет сменщики. И за рулём он настоящий ас! – заверил я.

– Ну, тогда сработаемся. Только не пойму, как вас пустили-то в таком спортивном наряде? У нас есть распорядок рабочего дня – вы с ним ознакомитесь, – сразу перешёл к делу Глеб Николаевич. – Тамара Алексеевна всё покажет и расскажет.

– Водители здесь тоже имеют дресс-код белых воротничков? – спросил Абдулваси.

– Да, форма одежды для всех одинаковая. Я вам дам подъёмные, купите костюмы и рубашки. Договорились? – спросил он.

– Хорошо, – ответил я.

Мы заметили, как Глеб Николаевич провожал заинтересованным взглядом каждую проходящую женщину за стеклянными стенами офиса. А служащие здесь были все как на подбор, такие красивые, стройные и элегантные. Мы с Абдулваси только головами покачивали. Шеф подмигнул нам и улыбнулся:

– Хотя бы посмотреть-то на эту красоту можно? Мужчина глазами должен быть сытым и ценить прекрасное. А так на работе ни-ни! Да я уж теперь старик Хотябыч.

Вам молодым этого не понять.

– Ну какой же вы старик? – в один голос возразили мы. – Зрелый мужчина в прекрасной форме!

Абдулваси всё же не удержался и пошутил:

– Просто Хотябыч или Хотимыч, но без возраста. А, Глеб Николаевич?

Шеф довольно рассмеялся:

– Молодец, Абдулваси, ловко словами играешь. А как тебя по батюшке величать? И насчёт образования поясни – что заканчивал?

Друг мой отчеканил:

– Адбулваси Абдулсалиевич, факультет русской филологии Таджикского госуниверситета.

– Здесь у нас принято всех по имени-отчеству называть. К твоему привыкнуть будет сложно, поэтому давай ты будешь Васи Салиевич. Не против?

– Все русские называют меня Вася.

– Ну тогда Василий Салиевич, что ли? – и обратился ко мне: – Фарход, а твоего отца как зовут?

– Папа у меня Гаффар. Получается Фарход Гаффарович, – ответил я.

– Вот и славненько. Давайте завтра с восьми часов на работу. Маршрут и адреса есть у Тамары Алексеевны. Ей же напишите заявления. Скоро праздники – корпоративы, работы будет много. Успеете выбрать одежду? Жить будете в пристройке моего загородного дома. Ну всё, на этом собеседование закончено.

Мы заторопились, ведь многое до завтра надо было успеть.

На этажах офиса мы хорошенько рассмотрели одежду сотрудников и решили поехать в ближайший универмаг. Увидели цены похожих костюмов и ахнули. Нет, рубашки мы взяли хорошие, аж по две штуки. Но костюм решили купить один на двоих. Да вот только по своим параметрам мы были очень разные. Я ниже и плотнее, а Абдулваси – выше и стройнее.

– Буду подгибать длину и никто не заметит, – деловито объяснил я другу.

– А я, как клоун, в коротких штанах и рукавах буду ходить? И ещё всё это на мне будет широко – пугало огородное! – возмутился Абдулваси.

– Ничего, до первой зарплаты потерпим. Нам ещё и по мелочам многое надо купить.

– Первым начнёшь работу ты, – серьёзно сказал мой друг. – Я не собираюсь клоуном за баранкой сидеть!

– Хорошо, Абдулваси! Поедем, надо выспаться. Мне в семь утра выезжать. А ты как раз разложишь вещи по местам, – примирительно ответил я.

Прежний водитель Доброва решил уехать к жене в Германию. Он объяснил, что к выезду шефа на работу машина должна быть заправлена, вымыта и быть на ходу, как часы. Штрафы гаишников будут высчитываться из нашей зарплаты.

Первый день прошёл на редкость удачно. Работы у меня было очень много, но особой усталости я не почувствовал. Глеб Николаевич, несмотря на занятость, всегда находил время пошутить и поддержать.

Я терзался мыслью, что будет, когда шеф заметит мой костюм. Но Глеб Николаевич искренне рассмеялся:

– Это почему ты взял костюм на вырост? Надеешься догнать Василия Салиевича? Давай в ателье – пусть тебе укоротят брюки и рукава, и обязательно поменяй обувь! Ты – тоже лицо моей компании!

Что мне было ответить?..

А когда на другой день шеф увидел Абдулваси в нашем общем костюме, то чуть со смеху не упал:

– Всё понятно, сэкономить решили? Нет, так не пойдёт. Поедете теперь за покупками вместе с Тамарой Алексеевной. Она научит вас имиджем дорожить.

Мой первый рабочий день был долгим, и всё же мне хотелось подготовить машину к завтрашнему рейсу Абдулваси. А он в моё отсутствие привёл в порядок и домик, и гараж.

– Ну как, не устал? – выйдя навстречу, спросил меня друг. И как всегда, не удержался от шутки:

– Целый день в руках баранку крутил, ну и не выдержал, съел?

– Об эту баранку, брат, все зубы обломаешь. Да и не позволит Глеб Николаевич на голодном пайке сидеть. Повезло нам с шефом, а?

– Да, хороший он человек, – согласился Абдулваси. – И фамилию свою оправдывает – точно Добров. А Старик Хоттабыч – волшебник из старого детского фильма, видно, его любимый герой. Не зря же Глеб Николаевич в шутку переименовал себя в старика

Хотябыча. Давай между нами оставим шефу это прозвище?

Я согласился:

– А что, даже прикольно – Добров старик Хотябыч! Он мне рассказывал, что вырос в Таджикистане и многих друзей там приобрёл. Ну и нас пригласил на работу к себе тоже вроде по-дружески.

– Доброву добром платим, – выдал эспромт Абдулваси.

В эту минуту у меня зазвонил телефон. Друг Абдулваси превратился весь в вопросительный знак.

– Старик Хотябыч вызывает. Поехали к шефу!

Лиха беда – начало!

– Интересно, для чего нас шеф вызвал в конце рабочего дня? – спросил меня Абдулваси.

– Наше дело успеть вовремя, Старик Хотябыч ждать не любит, – ответил я, садясь за руль. – Помчали!

– Фарход, не гони лошадёв! – Абдулваси опять не упустил случая перековеркать слова его любимого романса в исполнении Бориса Штоколова. Тут же включил диск с записью, и мощный бас повёл рассказ о ямщике, которому некуда больше спешить.

В проходной нас встретил начальник охраны Михаил Сергеевич Забиякин. Критически оглядел наши джинсы и белые рубашки, мол, опять не соблюли дресс-код и усмехнулся:

– По традиции мы представляем новых сотрудников всему коллективу.

Не переживайте, друзья, это просто знакомство.

Поднялись на восьмой этаж к конференц-залу, и прекрасная Тамара Алексеевна показала нам наши места. Сотрудники провожали новичков приветливыми взглядами и улыбками. Шеф Глеб Николаевич представил нас как старших водителей.

– Коллеги, прошу любить и жаловать – Василий Салиевич и Фарход Гаффарович. Кстати, мои земляки из Таджикистана. Думаю, сработаемся. Надо их поддержать, помочь побыстрее освоиться в нашем дружном коллективе. А вам, джигиты, желаю проявить себя профессионалами высшего класса.

И неожиданно добавил по-таджикски:

– Майли? Согласны?

В зале раздались удивлённые возгласы.

– Ташаккур, спасибо, Глеб Николаевич, не подведём! – в один голос заверили мы шефа.

На этом встреча закончилась. Добров отправился в свой кабинет, а сотрудники, прощаясь, подходили к нам и каждый стремился дружески пожать наши руки.

Выходили из здания вместе с Глебом Николаевичем и Забиякиным. Главный охранник тотчас заметил группу мигрантов, которых не пускали в офис.

– Похожи на наших таджиков-гастарбайтеров, – сказал шефу Абдулваси.

Глеб Николаевич тут же подошёл к ним выяснить в чём дело. Оказалось, что это рабочие-строители из Таджикистана. Они уже несколько дней ждали приезда Фаридуна, поэтому и разыскали меня, беспокоясь из-за его задержки.

– Михаил Сергеевич, пропустите всех в проходную, пусть Фарход пообщается со своими соотечественниками. А Василий Салиевич отвезёт меня по делам и вернётся за другом.

– Минуточку, Василий Салиевич, – сказал Забиякин, – один обязательный инструктаж!

– В случае опасности нажимаете эту кнопку, – он показал на незаметную кнопку под рулевой панелью и закрепил на карман рубашки бейджик «Василий Салиевич» с информацией о месте работы.

– Спасибо, Михаил Сергеевич, – сказал Адулваси, и они дружески пожали друг другу руки.

Я пошёл со своими земляками в проходную. Оказывается, ребята были из бригады нашего друга Фаридуна, который непонятно почему задерживался в Таджикистане. Работодатель определил срок: если завтра Фаридун не появится, он наймёт новую бригаду.

Куда же делся наш Фаридун? Неужели всё-таки решил провести соревнования борцов на праздновании по поводу обрезания сына?

Московский телефон Фаридуна был отключён. Я стал звонить в Ходжент, а он как будто ждал моего звонка.

Пришлось объяснить другу, что его работодатель ждёт только один день, иначе сменит бригаду. Фаридун заверил, что завтра же будет в Москве и расскажет о причине своей задержки. Ребята-земляки поблагодарили меня и обнадёженные отправились по домам.

А я остался ждать Абдулваси. Что-то долго его не было, похоже, в пробку попал. Вдруг вижу, ко мне спешит Забиякин:

– Быстро в машину, Фарход! У Василия Салиевича сработал механизм защиты.

Я сел рядом с Михаилом Сергеевичем и меня затрясло. В голове крутилась одна мысль – друг попал в беду. Что я скажу его родителям, жене и детям?

Забиякин, не поворачивая головы, скосил один глаз в мою сторону и неожиданно твёрдо, не блея, сказал:

– Спокойно, Фарход! Всё под контролем! – и включил камеру наблюдения. Мы увидели, как трое бритоголовых избивали двух мигрантов. Похоже, Абдулваси узнал своих таджиков – ещё пару секунд и скинхеды свалят их на землю и запинают до смерти. Абдулваси ловко въехал на тротуар, разделив машиной дерущихся. Мгновенно высунувшись в окно, он крикнул: «Бегите!»

Потерпевшие, утирая кровь с разбитых лиц, вмиг исчезли «с поля боя». Абдулваси с другой стороны широко распахнул дверь машины и с дружелюбной улыбкой сказал ошарашенным скинам:

– Не хотите прокатиться? Прошу!

Троица ринулась в салон. Главарь, играя пистолетом, ткнул в бейджик:

– Василий Салиевич? Чурка азиатская! Думаешь, ты герой? Будет у тебя лоб с дырой!

Второй бандит презрительно, словно выплёвывая слова, возразил:

– Ещё пулю на это дерьмо тратить! Выкинем его по дороге, а тачку клё-вую угоним, она нам пригодится.

А третий влез со своим предложением:

– Закопаем тебя, чурбана, никто и искать не будет. Развелось вас в Москве инородцев, как собак нерезаных. На каждом шагу – китайцы, кавказцы, узбеки, таджики, киргизы... А мы – патриоты России, санитары страны и всех вас перебьём!

– Гитлер тоже считал свою расу особенной, а что вышло? Не забыли историю? – возразил Абдулваси.

И тут кто-то из подонков кастетом ткнул в камеру, и изображение исчезло.

– Не переживай, Фарход, через двадцать минут машина остановится и датчики покажут, что нет бензина. Нам бы доехать побыстрее, а следом едут полицейские, – сказал Михаил Сергеевич.

Сигнал исчез. Мы снизили скорость, выключили фары и стали осматривать местность – дорога шла через лес. Сигнал подавался с левой стороны, на него мы и поехали.

Тихонько вышли из машины и увидели такую картину.

Наш Абдулваси рыл себе могилу и звучным голосом читал стихотворение Лермонтова:

В минуту жизни трудную
Теснится ль в сердце грусть:
Одну молитву чудную
Твержу я наизусть.
Есть сила благодатная
В созвучье слов живых,
И дышит непонятная,
Святая прелесть в них.

С души как бремя скатится,
Сомненье далеко –
И верится, и плачется,
И так легко, легко...

Я-то знал, что Абдулваси писал дипломную работу на тему «Стихи-молитвы известных русских поэтов», а вот Михаил Сергеевич был крайне удивлён.

С другой стороны дороги сидели три бритоголовых подонка и нетерпеливо смотрели на жертву. Главарь с вытянутым лицом и длинным носом был похож на Буратино. Второй, чисто рыжик – всё лицо в веснушках. Абдулваси точно бы про себя назвал его Конопатым. Третий – злобная рожа с ушами-локаторами, точно Ушастый.

Я крикнул другу:

– Абдулваси, чи хел? Как ты? – и подбежав, вырвал из его рук лопату, думая применить её для обороны.

– О-о-о! Ещё один чурка, да ещё с другом? Ты, дядя, чё – группа поддержки? Мы тебя вместе с ними уроем, – издевались наглецы.

Забиякин усмехнулся и пискнул:

– Береги нос, Буратино!

Наш Михаил Сергеевич видно не зря имел такую фамилию. Он крутанулся на месте, выкинул вверх свою ножищу с ботинком 46-го размера и вдарил пяткой прямо в нос вожака. Одновременно левым локтем ткнул Конопатого и ребром правой ладони резанул по шее Ушастого. Так нападавшие превратились в потерпевших. А Михаил Сергеевич уточнил:

– Кто ещё хочет пяткой в лобешник?

В ответ от поверженных раздались стоны и проклятья.

Я протянул Забиякину руку:

– Офарин, Михаил Сергеевич, то есть молодец! Спасибо, что моего друга выручили. Где вы служили?

– Спецназ, – коротко ответил Забиякин.

Тут подоспели полицейские на патрульной машине, а за ними и наш Добров. Я и не заметил, когда Забиякин успел позвонить шефу.

Скинхедов погрузили и повезли в отделение.

Забиякин подошёл к Доброву:

– Глеб Николаевич, может, я вас всех отвезу по домам? Джигитам-то надо прийти в себя после таких потрясений.

– Спасибо, Михаил Сергеевич, за службу и дружбу, – ответил Добров. – Фарход поведёт машину, а мы с Василием Салиевичем пассажирами побудем.

Забиякин кивнул и заторопился в офис. Мы сели в клёвую тачку, так и не доставшуюся подонкам, и покатили домой. Я по инерции включил диск с романсом Штоколова «Ямщик, не гони лошадей».

– Вот голос! – восхищённо сказал Добров. – Такой бас бы нашему Забиякину, а?

Я по привычке хихикнул, а Абдулваси с раскаянием поглядел на шефа:

– Глеб Николаевич, я ведь – дурбыляй, Михаила Сергеевича за его писклявый голос Заблиякиным назвал.

– Забиякин-Заблиякин? – захохотал Добров. – Ну ты даёшь, Василий Салиевич! В офисе об этом – никому. Понял?

– Понял, – ответил Абдулваси. – Только Михаил Сергеевич услышал обидную для него издёвку и даже виду не подал! А сегодня жизнью рисковал, чтобы меня выручить.

– Да уж! – согласился Добров. – Вот такая теперь у вас в Москве жизнь... Лиха беда – начало!

Царь-казан

Как вы уже знаете, друзья, из моих прошлых рассказов, жизнь наша оказалась полна приключений. Но скажу честно: мы с Абдулваси всегда стараемся любую неприятность разбавить шуткой. А вот наш Фаридун, есть за ним такой грех, из-за пустяков сразу впадает в панику. И начинает причитать: «Как быть? Такую жизнь врагу не пожелаешь...»

Приходится нам с Абдулваси на деле друга убеждать, что мир прекрасен, только нам самим надо его беречь и не разрушать походя.

Вот и на этот раз прилетел наш Фаридун в столицу с большим опозданием. А московский работодатель на стройке угрозу свою выполнил – уволил Фаридуна вместе с бригадой таджиков-гастарбайтеров и нанял других. В конце рабочего дня унылый наш друг пришёл в офис поделиться своей бедой.

А мы с Абдулваси в запарке – развозили на двух машинах иностранных гостей. Фаридун терпеливо ждал нас, сидя на лавочке у здания офиса. Наконец мы освободились. Друг имел жалкий вид и кусал губы, еле сдерживая слёзы. Я молча обнял его, а Абдулваси не обошёлся без допроса с пристрастием. Мы-то уже знали, что наши братья-таджики лишились прибыльного объекта из-за Фаридуна. Где их теперь устраивать? Подвёл Фаридун и себя самого, и рабочих.

А опоздал он в Москву из-за вызовов в суд. В Таджикистане у нас приняли (в целях экономии, что ли?) закон об ограничении финансовых затрат на обрядовые мероприятия и количество гостей. Мы с Абдулваси были на туе – обрезании сынишки Фаридуна и своими глазами видели, что никаких излишеств хозяин не позволил. Я уже рассказывал, что запланированное состязание борцов сорвал ливень. И даже мулла не вымолил у Бога солнышко на этот день ни в кредит, ни за наличные. Но нашёлся бдительный сосед и написал донос на Фаридуна, да ещё и фотографии предоставил «лишних зрителей». Те сидели на заборах, смотрели на праздник и хлопали в ладоши, а жена Фаридуна, добрая душа, ещё и угощала их сладостями. Вот дознаватели по головам их и посчитали, назначив Фаридуну большой штраф за нарушение закона.

Абдулваси не удержался от упрёка:

– Бог всё видит: деньги, которые ты хотел потратить на борцов, ушли на штраф. А если бы состязания всё-таки состоялись, то вдвое больше людей пришли поглядеть на них, а?

– Я в такие долги влез, приехал гол как сокол, а ты всё шутки шутишь, – обиделся на него друг.

– Гол в свои ворота! Вот как это называется! Теперь надо думать о трудоустройстве целой бригады. Если разбегутся, что будешь делать? – спросил я.

Фаридун опустил голову.

В это время из здания вышел Глеб Николаевич. Посмотрел на нас и спросил:

– Что за проблемы решаете? Никак ваш друг со всей бригадой остался без дела? Давайте знакомьте меня со своим бригадиром!

– Это наш Фаридун – «миллионер из трущоб». Решил всех удивить своим размахом по случаю обрезания сына. Теперь в долгах как в шелках, – ответил я.

– Ну, здравствуй, Фаридун! – дружелюбно протянул ему руку Глеб Николаевич. – Жду тебя завтра с утра, посмотрим, как можно вам помочь. Ты ребят из бригады не отпускай пока. Поехали, Фарход! А ты, Абдулваси, не бросай своего друга. Держитесь вместе.

Мы сели в машину, и Глеб Николаевич стал расспрашивать меня о Фаридуне: сколько лет он уже работает в Москве, каким строительством занимался, надёжные ли у него ребята в бригаде. Я всё рассказал. А шеф вдруг ответил стихами:

Сказал мудрец, в усах улыбку пряча:
Всё суета-сует и маята.
Есть у тебя дворец, счёт в банке, дача,
Но равнодушна вечности вода.

– Это я в студенческие годы стихами баловался. Пытался писать под восточного мудреца Мушфики. И сейчас это верно. Мы много суетимся, теряя какие-то человеческие качества.

– Вот ещё мой давний стих уместно вспомнить:

Единственный обмен вполне
Душою: я – тебе, ты – мне.

– Глеб Николаевич, очень похоже на наших восточных поэтов, – не удержался я от похвалы шефу. – Вы редкий человек и доброта ваша на всех изливается.

– Восточное воспитание, – откликнулся с улыбкой Добров. – А эти ваши обычаи знаю, целый год мужики работают, чтобы в один день всё потратить. Завтра посоветуемся, как можно помочь моему бедному соотечественнику.

И ещё рассказал, что сам родился и вырос в Душанбе, жил в Нуреке, где его дедушка работал заместителем начальника по строительству треста Нурек-ГЭСстрой:

– Меня многое связывает с Таджикистаном. Незабываемые воспоминания о добрых и отзывчивых людях! Даже не верится, что в солнечной мирной многонациональной республике могла случиться братоубийственная война...

На следующий день, после беседы с шефом Фаридун воспрял духом. Его бригаде поручили строительство загородных домов и дач для сотрудников фирмы.

Тамара Алексеевна, встретив меня на проходной, с улыбкой сказала:

– Ох, и любит Глеб Николаевич своих таджиков! Скоро у нас в компании все ваш язык освоят. Я, например, знаю, что обозначает слово «зебо» – красивая!

Я приложил руку к сердцу и поклонился нашей царице Тамаре. И тут меня позвал начальник охраны Забиякин:

– Фарход, Глеб Николаевич сказал, что ещё один Новый год есть у вас на Востоке. Хочет такой праздник в Москве провести, а подробности велел выяснить у тебя.

– Хоп, Михаил Сергеевич, давайте всё обсудим. По нашим традициям надо обязательно сделать настоящий плов в казане для всех сотрудников и гостей.

Навруз 21 марта выпал на рабочий день, и мы, посоветовавшись с шефом, перенесли праздник на выходные. Пригласили сотрудников на целый день с семьями и детьми.

Абдулваси срочно стал обзванивать наших друзей – певцов и музыкантов, без которых и Навруз не Навруз. Невестой праздника выбрали Тамару Алексеевну и попросили её прийти в белом и обязательно с восточной короной.

В бригаде Фаридуна был хороший повар, мы обязались ему помогать. У повара для больших мероприятий имелся свой казан литров на сорок. Привезли мы этот казан со стройки на машине. При разгрузке Фаридун решил отличиться.

Казан в перевёрнутом состоянии мы толкали из кузова машины. И вдруг на краю борта Фаридун, раскинув руки, как крылья, взялся за боковые ручки и решил один поставить его на землю. Но не рассчитал свои силы – казан упал, накрыв его, и звук тяжёлой махины раздался по всей округе. Мы испугались. Стали стучать по бокам казана и звать друга. Изнутри раздавались стоны. Мы поняли – Фаридун жив! Впятером перевернули казан и увидели: друг лежит на земле, свернувшись калачиком. Под наши вопли он тихо встал и показал на уши. Мы были рады, что он не покалечился, но похоже плохо слышал.

– В Москве Царь-пушка и Царь-колокол есть. Теперь и Царь-казан появился, да еще и Геракл-Фаридун при нём, – не удержался от шутки Абдулваси.

– А он и не слышит, казанный звон его оглушил. Надо к врачу! – строго сказал Михаил Сергеевич. – Вы займитесь подготовкой, а Фарход поедет с ним в травмпункт.

Слава Богу, у Фаридуна была просто небольшая «контузия». Врач уверил нас, что через недельку слух восстановится. Выписал лекарства и капли в уши.

Навруз прошёл весело. Красавица Тамара Алексеевна встречала всех как хозяйка праздника. Глеб Николаевич танцевал под таджикские ритмы, заражая всех весельем. Дети радостно бегали, играя друг с другом, малыши сидели с родителями, подростки читали стихи и пели, получая подарки из рук Фаридуна. Он сидел в сторонке от музыкантов и радовался, как ребёнок, ощущая себя Дедом Морозом.

В финале праздника Добров попросил меня и Абдулваси поздравить всех стихами на таджикском языке. Я прочитал народные четверостишья, а Абдулваси – рубаи Хайяма. Глеб Николаевич тоже вспомнил Хайяма на русском, а потом прочёл своё стихотворение:

Добро всегда прекрасно,
Оно не громогласно,
Тепло и искренне добро,
Уж таково его нутро.
Добра не ищут от добра,
А ждут с утра и до утра.
Добро купить никто не смог,
Ведь у него хозяин – Бог.

Праздник удался. Наши строители запели всем хорошо известную песню из кинофильма «Я встретил девушку», и участники стали с чувством подпевать.

Вот так и влились мы в московскую жизнь. Снова собрались вместе трое земляков из горного Таджикистана. Обрели хорошую работу, крышу над головой. А главное – добрых отзывчивых друзей, которые не делят людей по национальным признакам. О каждом из них хотелось бы рассказать подробно, с юмором и шуткой. Но это будут уже другие истории.

www.ingramcontent.com/pod-product-compliance
Lightning Source LLC
Chambersburg PA
CBHW081137300726
48982CB00006B/982

* 9 7 8 1 9 1 3 3 5 6 3 6 1 *